D0604359

THE JOY OF WALKING

More anthologies available from
Macmillan Collector's Library

Food for Thought

The Art of Solitude

Why Friendship Matters

THE JOY OF WALKING

Selected Writings

Edited and introduced by
SUZY CRIPPS

MACMILLAN COLLECTOR'S LIBRARY

This collection first published 2020 by Macmillan Collector's Library
an imprint of Pan Macmillan
The Smithson, 6 Briset Street, London EC1M 5NR
Associated companies throughout the world
www.panmacmillan.com

ISBN 978-1-5290-3264-2

Selection, introduction and author biographies © Suzy Cripps 2020

1 3 5 7 9 8 6 4 2

A CIP catalogue record for this book is available from the British Library.

Casing design and endpaper pattern by Andrew Davidson
Typeset in Plantin by Jouve (UK), Milton Keynes
Printed and bound in China by Imago

Visit www.panmacmillan.com to read more about all our books
and to buy them. You will also find features, author interviews and
news of any author events, and you can sign up for e-newsletters
so that you're always first to hear about our new releases.

Contents

Introduction
SUZY CRIPPS

'Never did I think so much, exist so vividly, and experience so much, never have I been so much myself, if I may dare to use the expression, as in the journeys I have taken alone and on foot.'

J. J. Rousseau, *The Confessions of Jean-Jacques Rousseau*

You have in your hands an anthology entitled *The Joy of Walking*. Perhaps you chose it because you're already a fully-fledged walker. In which case, welcome. I'm very happy that you're here. On the other hand, there's also a chance that you'd describe yourself as more of an indoors person. In your opinion, going out for a walk is nothing short of hell and, to you, 'the joy of walking' is a phrase loaded with irony. Walking, in your experience, has meant getting wet and cold in various rural locations. It's involved the misery of a sprained ankle or a blister. Or worse, an ill-fated school camping excursion, not dissimilar to *Lord of the Flies*, where you became hopelessly lost, split off into factions and got chased by a field of bullocks.

Perhaps, as a citizen of the postmodern world, you think that walking is fine for other people, but it isn't for you. As Henry Thoreau himself says in his popular essay 'Walking': *'Ambulator nascitur, non fit.'* That is, walkers are born and not made. There are two categories, you conclude: normal human beings, and walkers, the latter being an endangered species. But I think to categorize walking in this way is an oversight; to cut off the human being from walking is to discount the large majority of life for the large majority of humankind. Most of us walk, all the time, for all sorts of reasons, in all sorts of places.

For some, walking is a cure-all. A good friend recently showed me an amusing WhatsApp exchange with her mother, where, having dramatically lamented her troubles for several hundred words, she received a pragmatic, one-line response: 'Have a banana and go for a walk. x'. But it's a lot more than a form of therapy. Beyond walking being the practical function for getting where we need to be, we also walk to pass the time. A walk has a beginning, an end, an aim, it is a life in miniature. It gives us purpose. We walk to keep fit; many people obsessively track their steps from dawn till dusk. Some people walk miles every day to survive. Some people just walk to the corner shop.

Fine, you admit with the tired sigh of a soul that

has been dragged to one too many National Trust car parks, *it can't be denied that we do spend a large portion of our lives walking*. But is walking really *so* interesting a subject as to warrant an entire anthology?

It is undeniable that the simple act of putting one foot in front of the other has been an impetus for artistic expression throughout the course of human evolution. From the earliest days of literature written in English, walking has been quietly present: as a means of processing pain, as seen in the Old English poem 'The Wanderer', where the eponymous 'earth-stepper' treads the tracks of exile while pondering his grief, to the abundance of pilgrimage literature written in Middle English, where the physical journey facilitates a parallel journey of spiritual progress. What began in the Middle Ages has today evolved into a specific sub-genre, a literature of nature and walking (works such as Nan Shepherd's *The Living Mountain* or Robert Macfarlane's *The Old Ways* might spring to mind). Walking is intricately bound up in human existence. To pay attention to walking, then, is to pay attention to life itself, which seems like a valuable investment of time, to use the language of our day and age. I hope, however, that this anthology will suggest that walking often sublimates or distracts from the need for a 'return on investment'.

But how on earth do we begin to whittle down

our choices if literature about walking spans the centuries? It is obvious that anthologies require criteria or boundaries of some sort (if they are to be remotely portable, at least). The texts in this book span a period beginning in the mid seventeenth century to the early twentieth century. Aside from their already lionized status, these are texts that approach walking from a range of perhaps surprisingly different perspectives. Some of the extracts are from classic, cornerstone essays on walking; some are from novels, prompting us to think about walking as a rarely acknowledged spectre that exists quietly in, dare I say, most fiction. But first, we ought to warm up a little for our journey ahead, so let's take a brief tour of a few of the authors, texts and perspectives that we'll meet on the road.

In her brilliant history of pedestrianism, *Wanderlust*, Rebecca Solnit touches upon a key issue of contemporary life, that of hurry:

> I like walking because it is slow, and I suspect that the mind, like the feet, works at about three miles an hour. If this is so, then modern life is moving faster than the speed of thought or thoughtfulness.*

* Rebecca Solnit (2001), *Wanderlust: A History of Walking* (Penguin), p. 15.

We may be surprised that this seemingly very contemporary statement of walking as a mindful solution to a culture of hurry is echoed in the writing of authors from previous centuries. The eighteenth-century Welsh poet John Dyer praises the sweet relief brought about by the silence of walking into the countryside: 'Oh! pow'rful Silence! how you reign / In the poet's busy brain!' In fact, a great many of the poets, novelists and essayists in this anthology were great believers in the Latin adage *Mens sana in corpore sano*: 'a healthy mind in a healthy body'. We may nod specifically towards the seventeenth-century poet Thomas Traherne, who associated walking primarily with the mind: 'To walk is by a Thought to go; To mov in Spirit to and fro'. Similarly, our curiosity may be piqued by Walt Whitman's poem 'Song of the Open Road', where thought is represented as the fruit of walking: 'they hang there winter and summer on those trees and almost drop fruit as I pass'.

As well as a place for the cerebral, the reflective act of walking can soothe the emotions. Harriet Martineau notes in her autobiography that walking always left her with 'a cheered and lightened heart'. It can also stir up stronger passions. Thomas Hardy's narrator in 'At Castle Boterel', for example, relives the sensations of former romance as he retraces paths where he once walked with a lover. It goes without saying that walking and emotion were primary concerns of the Romantic era of poetry, represented in this anthology by Dorothy Wordsworth, John Clare, Robert Southey, Elizabeth Barrett Browning and William Wordsworth. For them, walking sometimes borders on a spiritual experience. Contrastingly, flights of the imagination are parodied in the brilliant Charlotte Lennox's *The Female Quixote*, as walking in the city excites the heroine to such an extent that she is unable to distinguish between fantasy and reality. Walking is a place for romance in this era, a rare space for privacy, as seen in Bathsheba Everdene and Sergeant Troy's meeting in the woods in *Far from the Madding Crowd*, or in Rosa Nouchette Carey's *Not Like Other Girls*, where Dick and Nan treasure their walks together.

Walking is, however, firstly and most evidently about movement. There is the latent possibility of venturing away from our quotidian, to 'close each book, drop each pursuit', as Jessie Redmon Fauset suggests in her poem 'Rondeau'. Walking, like travel, presents a sense of possibility, of spontaneity and of freedom. Walking offers us a chance to find the answer to a question that the young Cathy Earnshaw asks in Emily Brontë's *Wuthering Heights*: 'I wonder what lies on the other side'. Indeed, journeying on foot can give us a taste of what it might be like to depart from all our trappings. In Wilkie Collins's Cornish travelogue *Rambles Beyond Railways*, the author describes the walker becoming a kind of human tortoise, carrying around all their worldly goods in 'knapsacks, which now form part and parcel of their backs'. Walking, by definition, unless we have some kind of lackey, requires that we leave everything but the essentials of life behind.

Walking is not just about going on a long-distance hike in the manner of Collins. Many of the texts were chosen for their ability to describe accessible day-to-day acts of walking, recording the experiences of individuals who understand the vital and precious moments that walking can lead us into in everyday life. As Jenny Odell puts it so brilliantly in her book *How to Do Nothing* (2019), exploring is a vital aspect of strolling:

> wandering some unexpected secret passageway can feel like dropping out of linear time. Even if brief or momentary, these places and moments are retreats, and like longer retreats, they affect the way we see everyday life when we do come back to it.*

---

* Jenny Odell (2019), *How to Do Nothing: Resisting the Attention Economy* (Melville House), p. 9.

This means that both rural and urban walking can be of equal value in sustaining a lifestyle where we find regular refreshment and make new discoveries on foot. Christopher Morley boasted that he could find refreshing seclusion while walking the streets of Boston, claiming to be 'as solitary in a city street as ever Thoreau was in Walden'. More than that, there is great potential in walking in a city where a subliminal sense of adventure is always present when on foot. Lucy Snowe, the heroine of Charlotte Brontë's *Villette* (1853), thought that 'to walk alone in London seemed of itself an adventure'. In fact, the flâneur – a gentleman stroller who observes city life – became a literary trope in the nineteenth century. Charles Baudelaire gives a textbook example of the flâneur's escapades in his poem 'To a Passer-by', where the narrator describes his fleeting glance at a beautiful woman: 'Ah, how I drank, thrilled through like a Being insane, / In her look, a dark sky, from whence springs forth the hurricane.'

The city becomes a playground for the gentleman walker, providing him with a smorgasbord of sensory stimulation ready to be sampled. Modern scholarship has more recently pioneered the idea of the female equivalent (the flâneuse). However, walking the city has historically been considered a male occupation, a space viewed in literature primarily through the male gaze. For women, walking the streets was more commonly associated with selling your body.

Walking in general, in fact, was a white and male-dominated activity in the assorted historical contexts of this anthology. Henry Thoreau poses a pertinent question in his lecture 'Walking' when he talks about the fate of womankind in his day: 'How womankind, who are confined to the house still more than men, stand it I do not know; but I have ground to suspect that most of them do not *stand* it at all.'

He is right: the women in this anthology do not stand it, and so they walk. By and large, however, we notice that walking is written about and approached in a different way for women. It is not an aimless activity to pass the time, but one of the few methods of finding relief from the restrictions they face in society. Elizabeth Gaskell sums up this sentiment perfectly, referring to her protagonist Margaret Hale in *North and South*: 'Her out-of-doors life was perfect. Her in-doors life had its drawbacks.' Indeed, there can be an ecstasy in walking for women. Elizabeth Barrett Browning's Aurora roams the gardens of Leigh Hall feeling 'so young, so strong, so sure of God!' Outside this personal sense of fulfilment, however, the lifeline of pedestrianism is often met with responses of anxiety or disbelief. Many of these texts are a rebuttal to these kinds of voices. Be it Elizabeth Bennet's defiant (and muddy) walk to Netherfield Park in Jane Austen's *Pride and Prejudice* (1813), which is deemed 'silly' by her mother and 'incredible' by other women. Or Mrs Maple's sensible words in Fanny Burney's *The Wanderer*: 'What else has she got her feet for?' At any rate, the walking woman is a contentious figure.

Just as fewer women writers were published within the time frame of this anthology, the same applies to writers of colour. I have included some important texts: Rabindranath Tagore's letter collection *Glimpses of Bengal* (1885–1895) gives us a take on walking from the Indian sub-continent. I was also inspired by ideas in Camille T. Dungy's anthology *Black Nature: Four Centuries of African American Nature Poetry*, where the editor notes that nature writing by African American authors is often held captive by 'political' readings, when really, the corpus of work is far more thematically diverse.* To do this justice, I chose texts that offer different perspectives from African American writing in the era: firstly, an account of walking from *Narrative of the Life of Frederick Douglass, an American Slave* (1845).

---

* Camille T. Dungy (2009), *Black Nature: Four Centuries of African American Nature Poetry* (University of Georgia Press), p. xxiv.

It is included to provide some nuance to the idyllic picture of the world that is painted by more privileged authors in nineteenth-century walking literature. Secondly, I include Jessie Redmon Fauset's poem 'Rondeau' (1912) alongside this, because it is an example of African American writing about walking from the appropriate era that is not specifically considered to be a poem 'about race'. An anthology focusing on twentieth- and twenty-first-century accounts of walking could no doubt include a more diverse range of experiences. Nonetheless, the following texts give us a foundational insight into walking literature, broadly speaking from the English-speaking world, in the mid seventeenth to the early twentieth century.

It is my hope that you enjoy dipping in and out of the texts in this anthology. Perhaps that it might even inspire you to venture outside, after all, appreciating walking means paying attention to what is, for most, the cornerstone of existence, and thereby to the fact that you are alive. That seems worth exploring.

THE JOY OF WALKING

HENRY DAVID THOREAU
1817–1862

Henry David Thoreau was an American essayist, poet and philosopher. He was a proponent of Transcendentalism, a literary and philosophical movement whose core beliefs included the innate goodness of mankind and nature. Thoreau is best known for his book *Walden; or, Life in the Woods* (1854), which recounts his two years spent living in the forest. In the following extract from his lecture-turned-essay 'Walking' (1862), he explains how walking takes us away from civilization, forcing us to encounter both nature and our own selves.

from 'Walking'

> *"The West of which I speak is but another name for the Wild, and what I have been preparing to say is, that in wildness is the preservation of the world."*
>
> —THOREAU

> *"I believe in the forest, in the meadow, and in the night in which the corn grows."*
>
> —THOREAU

I wish to speak a word for Nature, for absolute freedom and wildness, as contrasted with a freedom and culture merely civil—to regard man as an inhabitant, or a part and parcel of Nature, rather than a member of society. I wish to make an extreme statement, if so I may make an emphatic one, for there are enough champions of civilization: the minister and the school committee, and every one of you will take care of that.

I have met with but one or two persons in the course of my life who understood the art of Walking, that is, of taking walks—who had a genius, so to speak, for *sauntering*: which word is beautifully derived "from idle people who roved about the country, in the Middle Ages, and asked charity, under pretence of going *à la Sainte Terre*," to the Holy Land, till the children exclaimed, "There goes a *Sainte-Terrer*,"

Saunterer—a Holy-Lander. They who never go to the Holy Land in their walks, as they pretend, are indeed mere idlers and vagabonds; but they who do go there are saunterers in the good sense, such as I mean. Some, however, would derive the word from *sans terre*, without land or a home, which therefore, in the good sense, will mean, having no particular home, but equally at home everywhere. For this is the secret of successful sauntering. He who sits still in a house all the time may be the greatest vagrant of all; but the saunterer, in the good sense, is no more vagrant than the meandering river, which is all the while sedulously seeking the shortest course to the sea. But I prefer the first, which indeed is the most probable derivation. For every walk is a sort of crusade, preached by some Peter the Hermit in us, to go forth and reconquer this Holy Land from the hands of the Infidels.

It is true we are but faint-hearted crusaders, even the walkers, nowadays, who undertake no persevering, never-ending enterprises. Our expeditions are but tours, and come round again at evening to the old hearth-side from which we set out. Half the walk is but retracing our steps. We should go forth on the shortest walk, perchance, in the spirit of undying adventure, never to return—prepared to send back our embalmed hearts only as relics to our desolate kingdoms. If you are ready to leave father and mother, and brother and sister, and wife and child and friends, and never see them again—if you have paid your debts, and made your will, and settled all your affairs, and are a free man, then you are ready for a walk.

To come down to my own experience, my companion and I, for I sometimes have a companion, take pleasure in fancying ourselves knights of a new, or rather an old, order—not Equestrians or Chevaliers, not Ritters or riders, but Walkers, a still more ancient and honourable class, I trust. The chivalric and heroic spirit which once belonged to the Rider seems now to reside in, or perchance to have subsided into, the Walker—not the Knight, but Walker Errant. He is a sort of fourth estate, outside of Church and State and People.

We have felt that we almost alone hereabouts practised this noble art; though, to tell the truth, at least if their own assertions are to be received, most of my townsmen would fain walk sometimes, as I do, but they cannot. No wealth can buy the requisite leisure, freedom, and independence, which are the capital in this profession. It comes only by the grace of God. It requires a direct dispensation from Heaven to become a walker. You must be born into the family of the Walkers. *Ambulator nascitur, non fit.* Some of my townsmen, it is true, can remember and have described to me some walks which they took ten years ago, in which they were so blessed as to lose themselves for half-an-hour in the woods; but I know very well that they have confined themselves to the highway ever since, whatever pretensions they may make to belong to this select class. No doubt they were elevated for a moment as by the reminiscence of a previous state of existence, when even they were foresters and outlaws.

> "When he came to grene wode,
> In a mery mornynge,
> There he herde the notes small
> Of byrdes mery syngynge.

> "It is ferre gone, sayd Robyn,
> That I was last here;
> Me lyste a lytell for to shote
> At the donne dere."

I think that I cannot preserve my health and spirits unless I spend four hours a day at least—and it is commonly more than that—sauntering through the woods and over the hills and fields, absolutely free from all worldly engagements. You may safely say, A penny for your thoughts, or a thousand pounds. When sometimes I am reminded that the mechanics and shopkeepers stay in their shops not only all the forenoon, but all the afternoon too, sitting with crossed legs, so many of them—as if the legs were made to sit upon, and not to stand or walk upon— I think that they deserve some credit for not having all committed suicide long ago.

I, who cannot stay in my chamber for a single day without acquiring some rust, and when sometimes I have stolen forth for a walk at the eleventh hour of four o'clock in the afternoon, too late to redeem the day, when the shades of night were already beginning to be mingled with the daylight, have felt as if I had committed some sin to be atoned for,—I confess that I am astonished at the power of endurance, to say nothing of the moral insensibility, of my neighbours who confine themselves to shops and offices the whole day for weeks and months, ay, and years almost together. I know not what manner of stuff they are of—sitting there now at three o'clock in the afternoon, as if it were three o'clock in the morning. Bonaparte may talk of the three-o'clock-in-the-morning courage, but it is nothing to the courage which can sit down cheerfully at this hour in the afternoon over against one's self whom you have known all the morning, to starve out a garrison to whom you are bound by such strong ties of sympathy. I wonder that about this time, or say between four and five o'clock in the afternoon, too late for the morning papers and too early for the evening ones, there is not a general explosion heard up and down the street, scattering a legion of antiquated and house-bred notions and whims to the four winds for an airing—and so the evil cure itself.

How womankind, who are confined to the house still more than men, stand it I do not know; but I have ground to suspect that most of them do not *stand* it at all. When, early in a summer afternoon, we have been shaking the dust of the village from the skirts of our garments, making haste past those houses with purely Doric or Gothic fronts, which have such an air of repose about them, my companion whispers that probably about these times their occupants are all gone to bed. Then it is that I appreciate the beauty and the glory of architecture, which itself never turns in, but for ever stands out and erect, keeping watch over the slumberers.

No doubt temperament, and, above all, age, have a good deal to do with it. As a man grows older, his ability to sit still and follow indoor occupations increases. He grows vespertinal in his habits as the evening of life approaches, till at last he comes forth only just before sundown, and gets all the walk that he requires in half-an-hour.

But the walking of which I speak has nothing in it akin to taking exercise, as it is called, as the sick

7

take medicine at stated hours—as the swinging of dumb-bells or chairs; but is itself the enterprise and adventure of the day. If you would get exercise, go in search of the springs of life. Think of a man's swinging dumb-bells for his health, when those springs are bubbling up in far-off pastures unsought by him!

Moreover, you must walk like a camel, which is said to be the only beast which ruminates when walking. When a traveller asked Wordsworth's servant to show him her master's study, she answered, "Here is his library, but his study is out of doors."

Living much out of doors, in the sun and wind, will no doubt produce a certain roughness of character—will cause a thicker cuticle to grow over some of the finer qualities of our nature, as on the face and hands, or as severe manual labour robs the hands of some of their delicacy of touch. So staying in the house, on the other hand, may produce a softness and smoothness, not to say thinness of skin, accompanied by an increased sensibility to certain impressions. Perhaps we should be more susceptible to some influences important to our intellectual and moral growth if the sun had shone and the wind blown on us a little less; and no doubt it is a nice matter to proportion rightly the thick and thin skin. But methinks that is a scurf that will fall off fast enough—that the natural remedy is to be found in the proportion which the night bears to the day, the winter to the summer, thought to experience. There will be so much the more air and sunshine in our thoughts. The callous palms of the labourer are conversant with finer tissues of self-respect and heroism, whose touch thrills the heart, than the languid fingers of idleness. That is mere sentimentality that lies abed by day and thinks itself white, far from the tan and callus of experience.

When we walk, we naturally go to the fields and woods: what would become of us if we walked only in a garden or a mall? Even some sects of philosophers have felt the necessity of importing the woods to themselves, since they did not go to the woods. "They planted groves and walks of Platanes," where they took *subdiales ambulationes* in porticos open to the air. Of course it is of no use to direct our steps to the woods if they do not carry us thither. I am alarmed when it happens that I have walked a mile into the woods bodily without getting there in spirit. In my afternoon walk I would fain forget all my morning occupations and my obligations to society. But it sometimes happens that I cannot easily shake off the village. The thought of some work will run in my head, and I am not where my body is—I am out of my senses. In my walks I would fain return to my senses. What business have I in the woods, if I am thinking of something out of the woods?

JOHN BURROUGHS
1837–1921

John Burroughs grew up on a rural farm in Delaware County, New York, and spent his childhood fascinated by the natural world around him. He went on to be a naturalist and an essayist, a friend of John Muir and Walt Whitman. In 'The Exhilarations of the Road' (1873), he describes the necessity of opting out of modern life from time to time in order to escape to the rural places where we truly belong. He asserts that the pedestrian 'is not merely a spectator of the panorama of nature but a participator in it'.

from 'The Exhilarations of the Road'

'Afoot and light-hearted I take to the open road.'
—WHITMAN

Occasionally on the sidewalk, amid the dapper, swiftly-moving, high-heeled boots and gaiters, I catch a glimpse of the naked human foot. Nimbly it scuffs along, the toes spread, the sides flatten, the heel protrudes; it grasps the curbing, or bends to the form of the uneven surfaces—a thing sensuous and alive, that seems to take cognizance of whatever it touches or passes. How primitive and uncivil it looks in such company—a real barbarian in the parlour. We are so unused to the human anatomy, to simple, unadorned nature, that it looks a little repulsive; but it is beautiful for all that. Though it be a black foot and an unwashed foot, it shall be exalted. It is a thing of life amid leather, a free spirit amid cramped, a wild bird amid caged, an athlete amid consumptives. It is the symbol of my order, the Order of Walkers. That unhampered, vitally playing piece of anatomy is the type of the pedestrian, man returned to first principles, in direct contact and intercourse with the earth and the elements, his faculties unsheathed, his mind plastic, his body toughened, his heart light, his soul dilated: while those cramped and distorted members in the calf and kid are the unfortunate wretches doomed to carriages and cushions.

I am not going to advocate the disuse of boots and shoes, or the abandoning of the improved modes of travel; but I am going to brag as lustily as I can on behalf of the pedestrian, and show how all the shining angels second and accompany the man who goes afoot, while all the dark spirits are ever looking out for a chance to ride.

When I see the discomforts that able-bodied American men will put up with rather than go a mile or half a mile on foot, the abuses they will tolerate and encourage, crowding the street car on a little fall in the temperature or the appearance of an inch or two of snow, packing up to overflowing, dangling to the straps, treading on each other's toes, breathing each other's breaths, crushing the women and children, hanging by tooth and nail to a square inch of the platform, imperilling their limbs and killing the horses—I think the commonest tramp in the street has good reason to felicitate himself on his rare privilege of going afoot. Indeed, a race that neglects or despises this primitive gift, that fears the touch of the soil, that has no footpaths, no community or ownership in the land which they imply, that warns off the walker as a trespasser, that knows no way bu the highway, the carriage-way, that forgets the stile, the foot-bridge, that even ignores the rights of the pedestrian in the public road, providing no escape for him but in the ditch or up the bank, is in a fair way to far more serious degeneracy.

Shakespeare makes the chief qualification of the walker a merry heart:—

> "Jog on, jog on, the foot-path way,
> And merrily hent the stile-a;
> A merry heart goes all the day,
> Your sad tires in a mile-a."

The human body is a steed that goes freest and longest under a light rider, and the lightest of all riders is a cheerful heart. Your sad, or morose, or embittered, or preoccupied heart settles heavily into the saddle, and the poor beast, the body, breaks down the first mile. Indeed, the heaviest thing in the world is a heavy heart. Next to that the most burdensome to the walker is a heart not in perfect sympathy and accord with the body—a reluctant or unwilling heart. The horse and rider must not only both be willing to go the same way, but the rider must lead the way and infuse his own lightness and eagerness into the steed. Herein is no doubt our trouble and one reason of the decay of the noble art in this country. We are unwilling walkers. We are not innocent and simple-hearted enough to enjoy a walk. We have fallen from that state of grace which capacity to enjoy a walk implies. It cannot be said that as a people we are so positively sad, or morose, or melancholic as that we are vacant of that sportiveness and surplusage of animal spirits that characterized our ancestors, and that springs from full and harmonious life—a sound heart in accord with a sound body. A man must invest himself near at hand and in common things, and be content with a steady and moderate return, if he would know the blessedness of a cheerful heart and the sweetness of a walk over the round earth. This is a lesson the American has yet to learn—capability of amusement on a low key. He expects rapid and extraordinary returns. He would make the very elemental laws pay usury. He has nothing to invest in a walk; it is too slow, too cheap. We crave the astonishing, the exciting, the far away, and do not know the highways of the gods when we see them—always a sign of the decay of the faith and simplicity of man.

If I say to my neighbour, "Come with me, I have great wonders to show you," he pricks up his ears and comes forthwith; but when I take him on the hills under the full blaze of the sun, or along the country road, our footsteps lighted by the moon and stars, and say to him, "Behold, these are the wonders, these are the circuits of the gods, this we now tread is a morning star," he feels defrauded, and as if I had played him a trick. And yet nothing less than dilatation and enthusiasm like this is the badge of the master walker.

If we are not sad we are careworn, hurried, discontented, mortgaging the present for the promise of the future. If we take a walk, it is as we take a prescription, with about the same relish and with about the same purpose; and the more the fatigue the greater our faith in the virtue of the medicine.

Of those gleesome saunters over the hills in spring, or those sallies of the body in winter, those excursions into space when the foot strikes fire at every step, when the air tastes like a new and finer mixture, when we accumulate force and gladness as we go along, when the sight of objects by the roadside and of the fields and woods pleases more than pictures or than all the art in the world—those ten or twelve mile dashes that are but the wit and effluence of the corporeal powers—of such diversion and open road entertainment, I say, most of us know very little.

I notice with astonishment that at our fashionable watering-places nobody walks; that of all those vast crowds of health-seekers and lovers of country air, you can never catch one in the fields or woods, or guilty of trudging along the country road with dust on his shoes and sun-tan on his hands and face. The sole amusement seems to be to eat and dress and sit about the hotels and glare at each other. The men look bored, the women look tired, and all seem to sigh, "O Lord! what shall we do to be happy and not be vulgar?" Quite different from our British cousins across the water, who have plenty of amusement and hilarity, spending most of the time at their watering-places in the open air, strolling, picnicking, boating, climbing, briskly walking, apparently with little fear of sun-tan or of compromising their "gentility".

It is indeed astonishing with what ease and hilarity the English walk. To an American it seems a kind of infatuation. When Dickens was in this country I imagine the aspirants to the honour of a walk with him were not numerous. In a pedestrian tour of England by an American, I read that "after breakfast with the Independent minister, he walked with us for six miles out of town upon our road. Three little boys and girls, the youngest six years old, also accompanied us. They were romping and rambling about all the while, and their morning walk must have been as much as fifteen miles; but they thought nothing of it, and when we parted were apparently as fresh as when they started, and very loath to return."

I fear, also, the American is becoming disqualified for the manly art of walking, by a falling off in the size of his foot. He cherishes and cultivates this part of his anatomy, and apparently thinks his taste and good breeding are to be inferred from its diminutive size. A small, trim foot, well booted or gaitered, is the national vanity. How we stare at the big feet of foreigners, and wonder what may be the price of leather in those countries, and where all the aristocratic blood is, that these plebeian extremities so predominate. If we were admitted to the confidences of the shoemaker to Her Majesty or to His Royal Highness, no doubt we would modify our views upon this latter point, for a truly large and royal nature is never stunted in the extremities; a little foot never yet supported a great character.

CHARLOTTE BRONTË
1816–1855

Charlotte Brontë was the eldest of the three Brontë sisters who survived to adulthood, all of whom were novelists. She grew up in a parsonage in rural Yorkshire, spending a significant part of her childhood playing on the local moors. In her novel *Villette* (1853), the narrator Lucy Snowe describes an overpowering feeling of liberation as she roams the streets of London for the first time. Walking through the city provides a sense of opportunity and excitement for the sheltered Victorian woman.

from *Villette*

CHAPTER VI

LONDON

The next day was the first of March, and when I awoke, rose, and opened my curtain, I saw the risen sun struggling through fog. Above my head, above the house-tops, co-elevate almost with the clouds, I saw a solemn, orbed mass, dark-blue and dim—THE DOME. While I looked, my inner self moved; my spirit shook its always-fettered wings half loose; I had a sudden feeling as if I, who never yet truly lived, were at last about to taste life. In that morning my soul grew as fast as Jonah's gourd.

"I did well to come," I said, proceeding to dress with speed and care. "I like the spirit of this great London which I feel around me. Who but a coward would pass his whole life in hamlets, and for ever abandon his faculties to the eating rust of obscurity?"

Being dressed, I went down; not travel-worn and exhausted, but tidy and refreshed. When the waiter came in with my breakfast, I managed to accost him sedately, yet cheerfully; we had ten minutes' discourse, in the course of which we became usefully known to each other.

He was a grey-haired, elderly man; and, it seemed, had lived in his present place twenty years.

Having ascertained this, I was sure he must remember my two uncles, Charles and Wilmot, who, fifteen years ago, were frequent visitors here. I mentioned their names; he recalled them perfectly, and with respect. Having intimated my connection, my position in his eyes was henceforth clear, and on a right footing. He said I was like my uncle Charles: I suppose he spoke truth, because Mrs Barrett was accustomed to say the same thing. A ready and obliging courtesy now replaced his former uncomfortably doubtful manner; henceforth I need no longer be at a loss for a civil answer to a sensible question.

The street on which my little sitting-room window looked was narrow, perfectly quiet, and not dirty: the few passengers were just such as one sees in provincial towns: here was nothing formidable; I felt sure I might venture out alone.

Having breakfasted, out I went. Elation and pleasure were in my heart: to walk alone in London seemed of itself an adventure. Presently I found myself in Paternoster Row—classic ground this. I entered a bookseller's shop, kept by one Jones: I bought a little book—a piece of extravagance I could ill afford; but I thought I would one day give or send it to Mrs Barrett. Mr Jones, a dried-in man of business, stood behind his desk: he seemed one of the greatest, and I one of the happiest of beings.

Prodigious was the amount of life I lived that morning. Finding myself before St Paul's, I went in; I mounted to the dome: I saw thence London, with its river, and its bridges, and its churches; I saw antique Westminster, and the green Temple Gardens, with sun upon them, and a glad, blue sky, of early spring above; and, between them and it, not too dense a cloud of haze.

Descending, I went wandering whither chance might lead, in a still ecstasy of freedom and enjoyment; and I got—I know not how—I got into the heart of city life. I saw and felt London at last: I got into the Strand; I went up Cornhill; I mixed with the life passing along; I dared the perils of crossings. To do this, and to do it utterly alone, gave me, perhaps an irrational, but a real pleasure. Since those days, I have seen the West-end, the parks, the fine squares; but I love the city far better. The city seems so much more in earnest: its business, its rush, its roar, are such serious things, sights, and sounds. The city is getting its living—the West-end but enjoying its pleasure. At the West-end you may be amused, but in the city you are deeply excited.

Faint, at last, and hungry (it was years since I had felt such healthy hunger), I returned, about two o'clock, to my dark, old, and quiet inn. I dined on two dishes—a plain joint, and vegetables; both seemed excellent: how much better than the small, dainty messes Miss Marchmont's cook used to send up to my kind, dead mistress and me, and to the discussion of which we could not bring half an appetite between us! Delightfully tired, I lay down on three chairs for an hour (the room did not boast a sofa). I slept, then I woke and thought for two hours.

My state of mind, and all accompanying circumstances, were just now such as most to favour the adoption of a new, resolute, and daring—perhaps desperate—line of action. I had nothing to lose. Unutterable loathing of a desolate existence past, forbade return. If I failed in what I now designed to undertake, who, save myself, would suffer? If I died far away from—home, I was going to say, but I had no home—from England, then, who would weep?

I might suffer; I was inured to suffering: death itself had not, I thought, those terrors for me which it has for the softly reared. I had, ere this, looked on the thought of death with a quiet eye. Prepared, then, for any consequences, I formed a project.

E. M. FORSTER
1879–1970

Edward Morgan Forster was an English novelist and essayist who was nominated for the Nobel Prize in Literature on sixteen occasions. His work poses questions about conformity and socially conditioned behaviours. In this extract from his third novel, *A Room with a View* (1908), walking without a Baedeker guidebook symbolizes moving away from the beaten track of socially acceptable behaviour and into the unknown paths of natural impulse. Lucy Honeychurch finds herself having to navigate the streets of Florence without Baedeker to tell her where to go and what to think. Exploring Florence independently is her first step in learning to make her own choices, which will lead to her own personal Renaissance by the end of the novel.

from *A Room with a View*

"Bless us! Bless us and save us! We've lost the way."

Certainly they had seemed a long time in reaching Santa Croce, the tower of which had been plainly visible from the landing window. But Miss Lavish had said so much about knowing her Florence by heart, that Lucy had followed her with no misgivings.

"Lost! lost! My dear Miss Lucy, during our political diatribes we have taken a wrong turning. How those horrid Conservatives would jeer at us! What are we to do? Two lone females in an unknown town. Now, this is what *I* call an adventure."

Lucy, who wanted to see Santa Croce, suggested, as a possible solution, that they should ask the way there.

"Oh, but that is the word of a craven! And no, you are not, not, *not* to look at your Baedeker. Give it to me; I shan't let you carry it. We will simply drift."

Accordingly they drifted through a series of those grey-brown streets, neither commodious nor picturesque, in which the eastern quarter of the city abounds. Lucy soon lost interest in the discontent of Lady Louisa, and became discontented herself. For one ravishing moment Italy appeared. She stood in the Square of the Annunziata and saw in the living terra-cotta those divine babies whom no cheap reproduction can ever stale. There they stood, with their shining limbs bursting from the garments of charity, and their strong white arms extended against circlets of heaven. Lucy thought she had never seen anything more beautiful; but Miss Lavish, with a shriek of dismay, dragged her forward, declaring that they were out of their path now by at least a mile.

The hour was approaching at which the continental breakfast begins, or rather ceases, to tell, and the ladies bought some hot chestnut paste out of a little shop, because it looked so typical. It tasted partly of the paper in which it was wrapped, partly of hair-oil, partly of the great unknown. But it gave them strength to drift into another Piazza, large and dusty, on the farther side of which rose a black-and-white façade of surpassing ugliness. Miss Lavish spoke to it dramatically. It was Santa Croce. The adventure was over.

"Stop a minute; let those two people go on, or I shall have to speak to them. I do detest conventional intercourse. Nasty! they are going into the church, too. Oh, the Britisher abroad!"

"We sat opposite them at dinner last night. They have given us their rooms. They were so very kind."

"Look at their figures!" laughed Miss Lavish.

"They walk through my Italy like a pair of cows. It's very naughty of me, but I would like to set an examination paper at Dover, and turn back every tourist who couldn't pass it."

"What would you ask us?"

Miss Lavish laid her hand pleasantly on Lucy's arm, as if to suggest that she, at all events, would get full marks. In this exalted mood they reached the steps of the great church, and were about to enter it when Miss Lavish stopped, squeaked, flung up her arms, and cried:

"There goes my local-colour box! I must have a word with him!"

And in a moment she was away over the Piazza, her military cloak flapping in the wind; nor did she slacken speed till she caught up an old man with white whiskers, and nipped him playfully upon the arm.

Lucy waited for nearly ten minutes. Then she began to get tired. The beggars worried her, the dust blew in her eyes, and she remembered that a young girl ought not to loiter in public places. She descended slowly into the Piazza with the intention of rejoining Miss Lavish, who was really almost too original. But at that moment Miss Lavish and her local-colour box moved also, and disappeared down a side street, both gesticulating largely.

Tears of indignation came to Lucy's eyes—partly because Miss Lavish had jilted her, partly because she had taken her Baedeker. How could she find her way home? How could she find her way about in Santa Croce? Her first morning was ruined, and she might never be in Florence again. A few minutes ago she had been all high spirits, talking as a woman of culture, and half persuading herself that she was full of originality. Now she entered the church depressed and humiliated, not even able to remember whether it was built by the Franciscans or the Dominicans.

Of course, it must be a wonderful building. But how like a barn! And how very cold! Of course, it contained frescoes by Giotto, in the presence of whose tactile values she was capable of feeling what was proper. But who was to tell her which they were? She walked about disdainfully, unwilling to be enthusiastic over monuments of uncertain author-ship or date. There was no one even to tell her which, of all the sepulchral slabs that paved the nave and transepts, was the one that was really beautiful, the one that had been most praised by Mr. Ruskin.

Then the pernicious charm of Italy worked on her, and, instead of acquiring information, she began to be happy. She puzzled out the Italian notices—the notice that forbade people to introduce dogs into the church—the notice that prayed people, in the interests

27

of health and out of respect to the sacred edifice in which they found themselves, not to spit. She watched the tourists; their noses were as red as their Baedekers, so cold was Santa Croce. She beheld the horrible fate that overtook three Papists—two he-babies and a she-baby—who began their career by sousing each other with the Holy Water, and then proceeded to the Machiavelli memorial, dripping, but hallowed. Advancing towards it very slowly and from immense distances, they touched the stone with their fingers, with their handkerchiefs, with their heads, and then retreated. What could this mean? They did it again and again. Then Lucy realized that they had mistaken Machiavelli for some saint, and by continual contact with his shrine were hoping to acquire virtue. Punishment followed quickly. The smallest he-baby stumbled over one of the sepulchral slabs so much admired by Mr. Ruskin, and entangled his feet in the features of a recumbent bishop. Protestant as she was, Lucy darted forward. She was too late. He fell heavily upon the prelate's upturned toes.

"Hateful bishop!" exclaimed the voice of old Mr. Emerson, who had darted forward also. "Hard in life, hard in death. Go out into the sunshine, little boy, and kiss your hand to the sun, for that is where you ought to be. Intolerable bishop!"

The child screamed frantically at these words,

and at these dreadful people who picked him up, dusted him, rubbed his bruises, and told him not to be superstitious.

"Look at him!" said Mr. Emerson to Lucy. "Here's a mess: a baby hurt, cold, and frightened! But what else can you expect from a church?"

The child's legs had become as melting wax. Each time that old Mr. Emerson and Lucy set it erect it collapsed with a roar. Fortunately an Italian lady, who ought to have been saying her prayers, came to the rescue. By some mysterious virtue, which mothers alone possess, she stiffened the little boy's backbone and imparted strength to his knees. He stood. Still gibbering with agitation, he walked away.

"You are a clever woman," said Mr. Emerson. "You have done more than all the relics in the world. I am not of your creed, but I do believe in those who make their fellow-creatures happy. There is no scheme of the universe—"

He paused for a phrase.

"*Niente*," said the Italian lady, and returned to her prayers.

"I'm not sure she understands English," suggested Lucy.

In her chastened mood she no longer despised the Emersons. She was determined to be gracious to

29

them, beautiful rather than delicate, and, if possible, to erase Miss Bartlett's civility by some gracious reference to the pleasant rooms.

"That woman understands everything," was Mr. Emerson's reply. "But what are you doing here? Are you doing the church? Are you through with the church?"

"No," cried Lucy, remembering her grievance. "I came here with Miss Lavish, who was to explain everything; and just by the door—it is too bad!—she simply ran away, and after waiting quite a time, I had to come in by myself."

"Why shouldn't you?" said Mr. Emerson.

"Yes, why shouldn't you come by yourself?" said the son, addressing the young lady for the first time.

"But Miss Lavish has even taken away Baedeker."

"Baedeker?" said Mr. Emerson. "I'm glad it's *that* that you minded. It's worth minding, the loss of a Baedeker. *That's* worth minding."

Lucy was puzzled. She was again conscious of some new idea, and was not sure whither it would lead her.

"If you've no Baedeker," said the son, "you'd better join us."

Was this where the idea would lead? She took refuge in her dignity.

"Thank you very much, but I could not think of that. I hope you do not suppose that I came to join on to you. I really came to help with the child, and to thank you for so kindly giving us your rooms last night. I hope that you have not been put to any great inconvenience."

"My dear," said the old man gently, "I think that you are repeating what you have heard older people say. You are pretending to be touchy; but you are not really. Stop being so tiresome, and tell me instead what part of the church you want to see. To take you to it will be a real pleasure."

ROBERT LOUIS STEVENSON
1850–1894

Robert Louis Stevenson was a Scottish writer, best known for his novels *Treasure Island* (1883) and *The Strange Case of Dr Jekyll and Mr Hyde* (1886). Stevenson's literary career began as a travel writer, where he recounted his real-life journeys in *An Inland Voyage* (1878) and *Travels with a Donkey in the Cévennes* (1879). The following extract is from his essay 'Walking Tours' (1876), which was inspired by William Hazlitt's essay, 'On Going a Journey'. It details the simple peace and pleasure of journeying alone.

from 'Walking Tours'

It must not be imagined that a walking tour, as some would have us fancy, is merely a better or worse way of seeing the country. There are many ways of seeing landscape quite as good; and none more vivid, in spite of canting dilettanti, than from a railway train. But landscape on a walking tour is quite accessory. He who is indeed of the brotherhood does not voyage in quest of the picturesque, but of certain jolly humours—of the hope and spirit with which the march begins at morning, and the peace and spiritual repletion of the evening's rest. He cannot tell whether he puts his knapsack on, or takes it off, with more delight. The excitement of the departure puts him in key for that of the arrival. Whatever he does is not only a reward in itself, but will be further rewarded in the sequel; and so pleasure leads on to pleasure in an endless chain. It is this that so few can understand; they will either be always lounging or always at five miles an hour; they do not play off the one against the other, prepare all day for the evening, and all evening for the next day. And, above all, it is here that your overwalker fails of comprehension. His heart rises against those who drink their curaçao in liqueur glasses, when he himself can swill it in a brown John. He will not believe that the flavour

33

is more delicate in the smaller dose. He will not believe that to walk this unconscionable distance is merely to stupefy and brutalise himself, and come to his inn, at night, with a sort of frost on his five wits, and a starless night of darkness in his spirit. Not for him the mild luminous evening of the temperate walker! He has nothing left of man but a physical need for bedtime and a double nightcap; and even his pipe, if he be a smoker, will be savourless and disenchanted. It is the fate of such an one to take twice as much trouble as is needed to obtain happiness, and miss the happiness in the end; he is the man of the proverb, in short, who goes further and fares worse.

Now, to be properly enjoyed, a walking tour should be gone upon alone. If you go in a company, or even in pairs, it is no longer a walking tour in anything but name; it is something else and more in the nature of a picnic. A walking tour should be gone upon alone, because freedom is of the essence; because you should be able to stop and go on, and follow this way or that, as the freak takes you; and because you must have your own pace, and neither trot alongside a champion walker, nor mince in time with a girl. And then you must be open to all impressions and let your thoughts take colour from what you see. You should be as a pipe for any wind to play

34

upon. "I cannot see the wit," says Hazlitt, "of walking and talking at the same time. When I am in the country I wish to vegetate like the country,"—which is the gist of all that can be said upon the matter. There should be no cackle of voices at your elbow, to jar on the meditative silence of the morning. And so long as a man is reasoning he cannot surrender himself to that fine intoxication that comes of much motion in the open air, that begins in a sort of dazzle and sluggishness of the brain, and ends in a peace that passes comprehension.

During the first day or so of any tour there are moments of bitterness, when the traveller feels more than coldly towards his knapsack, when he is half in a mind to throw it bodily over the hedge and, like Christian on a similar occasion, "give three leaps and go on singing." And yet it soon acquires a property of easiness. It becomes magnetic; the spirit of the journey enters into it. And no sooner have you passed the straps over your shoulder than the lees of sleep are cleared from you, you pull yourself together with a shake, and fall at once into your stride. And surely, of all possible moods, this, in which a man takes the road, is the best.

WALT WHITMAN
1819–1892

Walt Whitman was an American poet and essayist. His 1855 poetry collection *Leaves of Grass* is considered to be a groundbreaking text in American literary history, although his overt descriptions of sensuality and his stylistic innovations caused great controversy and confusion at the time. Heavily influenced by transcendentalist philosophy, Whitman wrote poetry that celebrated the vital connection between mankind and nature. It is therefore no surprise that he should produce a poem like 'Song of the Open Road' (1856), which describes an ecstatic unbridled joy as the narrator journeys on foot through town and country.

from 'Song of the Open Road'

I

Afoot and light-hearted I take to the open road,
Healthy, free, the world before me,
The long brown path before me leading wherever
    I choose.

Henceforth I ask not good-fortune, I myself am
    good-fortune,
Henceforth I whimper no more, postpone no more,
    need nothing,
Done with indoor complaints, libraries, querulous
    criticisms,
Strong and content I travel the open road.

The earth, that is sufficient,
I do not want the constellations any nearer,
I know they are very well where they are,
I know they suffice for those who belong to them.

(Still here I carry my old delicious burdens,
I carry them, men and women, I carry them with me
    wherever I go,
I swear it is impossible for me to get rid of them,
I am fill'd with them, and I will fill them in return.)

4

The earth expanding right hand and left hand,
The picture alive, every part in its best light,
The music falling in where it is wanted, and stopping
    where it is not wanted,
The cheerful voice of the public road, the gay fresh
    sentiment of the road.

O highway I travel, do you say to me *Do not
    leave me?*
Do you say *Venture not—if you leave me you are lost?*
Do you say *I am already prepared, I am well beaten and
    undenied, adhere to me?*

O public road, I say back I am not afraid to leave you,
    yet I love you,
You express me better than I can express myself,
You shall be more to me than my poem.

I think heroic deeds were all conceiv'd in the open air,
    and all free poems also,
I think I could stop here myself and do miracles,
I think whatever I meet on the road I shall like,
    and whoever beholds me shall like me,
I think whoever I see must be happy.

From this hour I ordain myself loos'd of limits and
    imaginary lines,
Going where I list, my own master total and absolute,
Listening to others, considering well what they say,
Pausing, searching, receiving, contemplating,
Gently, but with undeniable will, divesting myself of the
    holds that would hold me.

I inhale great draughts of space,
The east and the west are mine, and the north and the
    south are mine.

I am larger, better than I thought,
I did not know I held so much goodness.

All seems beautiful to me,
I can repeat over to men and women You have done such
    good to me I would do the same to you,
I will recruit for myself and you as I go,
I will scatter myself among men and women as I go,
I will toss a new gladness and roughness among them,
Whoever denies me it shall not trouble me,
Whoever accepts me he or she shall be blessed and shall
    bless me.

Now if a thousand perfect men were to appear it would
    not amaze me,

Now if a thousand beautiful forms of women appear'd
    it would not astonish me.

Now I see the secret of the making of the best
    persons,

It is to grow in the open air and eat and sleep with
    the earth.

Here a great personal deed has room,

(Such a deed seizes upon the hearts of the whole race
    of men,

Its effusion of strength and will overwhelms laws and
    mocks all authority and all argument against it.)

Here is the test of wisdom,

Wisdom is not finally tested in schools,

Wisdom cannot be pass'd from one having it to another
    not having it,

Wisdom is of the soul, is not susceptible of proof,
    is its own proof,

Applies to all stages and objects and qualities and is
    content,

Is the certainty of the reality and immortality of things,
    and the excellence of things;

Something there is in the float of the sight of things
    that provokes it out of the soul.

Now I re-examine philosophies and religions,
They may prove well in lecture-rooms, yet not prove at
    all under the spacious clouds and along the
    landscape and flowing currents.

Here is realization,
Here is a man tallied—he realizes here what he has
    in him,
The past, the future, majesty, love—if they are vacant
    of you, you are vacant of them.

Only the kernel of every object nourishes;
Where is he who tears off the husks for you and me?
Where is he that undoes stratagems and envelopes for
    you and me?

Here is adhesiveness, it is not previously fashion'd, it is
    apropos;
Do you know what it is as you pass to be loved by
    strangers?
Do you know the talk of those turning eye-balls?

7

Here is the efflux of the soul,

The efflux of the soul comes from within through
      embower'd gates, ever provoking questions,

These yearnings why are they? these thoughts in the
      darkness why are they?

Why are there men and women that while they are nigh
      me the sunlight expands my blood?

Why when they leave me do my pennants of joy sink flat
      and lank?

Why are there trees I never walk under but large and
      melodious thoughts descend upon me?

(I think they hang there winter and summer on those
      trees and almost drop fruit as I pass;)

What is it I interchange so suddenly with strangers?

What with some driver as I ride on the seat by his side?

What with some fisherman drawing his seine by the shore
      as I walk by and pause?

What gives me to be free to a woman's and man's
      good-will? what gives them to be free to mine?

8

The efflux of the soul is happiness, here is happiness,

I think it pervades the open air, waiting at all times,

Now it flows unto us, we are rightly charged.

Here rises the fluid and attaching character,

The fluid and attaching character is the freshness and
    sweetness of man and woman,
(The herbs of the morning sprout no fresher and sweeter
    every day out of the roots of themselves, than it
    sprouts fresh and sweet continually out of itself.)

Toward the fluid and attaching character exudes the
    sweat of the love of young and old,
From it falls distill'd the charm that mocks beauty and
    attainments,
Toward it heaves the shuddering longing ache of
    contact.

13

Allons! to that which is endless as it was beginningless,
To undergo much, tramps of days, rests of nights,
To merge all in the travel they tend to, and the days and
    nights they tend to,
Again to merge them in the start of superior journeys,
To see nothing anywhere but what you may reach it and
    pass it,
To conceive no time, however distant, but what you may
    reach it and pass it,
To look up or down the road but it stretches and waits
    for you, however long but it stretches and waits
    for you,

43

To see no being, not God's or any, but you also go
     thither,
To see no possession but may possess it, enjoying all
     without labour or purchase, abstracting the feast yet
     not abstracting one particle of it,
To take the best of the farmer's farm and the rich
     man's elegant villa, and the chaste blessings of the
     well-married couple, and the fruits of orchards and
     flowers of gardens,
To take to your use out of the compact cities as you pass
     through,
To carry buildings and streets with you afterward
     wherever you go,
To gather the minds of men out of their brains as you
     encounter them, to gather the love out of their
     hearts,
To take your lovers on the road with you, for all that you
     leave them behind you,
To know the universe itself as a road, as many roads, as
     roads for travelling souls.

All parts away for the progress of souls,
All religion, all solid things, arts, governments—all
     that was or is apparent upon this globe or any
     globe, falls into niches and corners before the
     procession of souls along the grand roads of the
     universe.

Of the progress of the souls of men and women along the
    grand roads of the universe, all other progress is the
    needed emblem and sustenance.

Forever alive, forever forward,
Stately, solemn, sad, withdrawn, baffled, mad, turbulent,
    feeble, dissatisfied,
Desperate, proud, fond, sick, accepted by men, rejected
    by men,
They go! they go! I know that they go, but I know not
    where they go,
But I know that they go toward the best—toward
    something great.

Whoever you are, come forth! or man or woman come
    forth!
You must not stay sleeping and dallying there in the
    house, though you built it, or though it has been
    built for you.

Out of the dark confinement! out from behind the
    screen!
It is useless to protest, I know all and expose it.

Behold through you as bad as the rest,
Through the laughter, dancing, dining, supping, of
    people,

Inside of dresses and ornaments, inside of those wash'd
and trimm'd faces,

Behold a secret silent loathing and despair.

No husband, no wife, no friend, trusted to hear the
confession,

Another self, a duplicate of every one, skulking and
hiding it goes,

Formless and wordless through the streets of the cities,
polite and bland in the parlours,

In the cars of railroads, in steamboats, in the public
assembly,

Home to the houses of men and women, at the table,
in the bed-room, everywhere,

Smartly attired, countenance smiling, form upright, death
under the breast-bones, hell under the skull-bones,

Under the broadcloth and gloves, under the ribbons and
artificial flowers,

Keeping fair with the customs, speaking not a syllable of
itself,

Speaking of anything else, but never of itself.

15

Allons! the road is before us!

It is safe—I have tried it—my own feet have tried it
well—be not detain'd!

Let the paper remain on the desk unwritten, and the
    book on the shelf unopen'd!
Let the tools remain in the workshop! let the money
    remain unearn'd!
Let the school stand! mind not the cry of the teacher!
Let the preacher preach in his pulpit! let the lawyer plead
    in the court, and the judge expound the law.

Camerado, I will give you my hand!
I give you my love more precious than money,
I give you myself before preaching or law;
Will you give me yourself? will you come travel with me?
Shall we stick by each other as long as we live?

WILLIAM HAZLITT
1778–1830

William Hazlitt was a literary critic and essayist, chiefly remembered today for his acquaintance with and writings about the Romantic poets. In 'On Going a Journey' (1821) he writes about the joy of walking alone, without any human companion. The piece later inspired Robert Louis Stevenson, who responded directly to it in his own essay 'Walking Tours', where he describes Hazlitt's essay as 'so good that there should be a tax levied on all who have not read it'. It is a wonderful reminder of the fruitfulness of solitude.

from 'On Going a Journey'

One of the pleasantest things in the world is going a journey; but I like to go by myself. I can enjoy society in a room; but out of doors, nature is company enough for me. I am then never less alone than when alone.

> "The fields his study, nature was his book."

I cannot see the wit of walking and talking at the same time. When I am in the country, I wish to vegetate like the country. I am not for criticising hedge-rows and black cattle. I go out of town in order to forget the town and all that is in it. There are those who for this purpose go to watering-places, and carry the metropolis with them. I like more elbow-room, and fewer incumbrances. I like solitude, when I give myself up to it, for the sake of solitude; nor do I ask for

> "—a friend in my retreat,
> Whom I may whisper, solitude is sweet."

The soul of a journey is liberty, perfect liberty, to think, feel, do just as one pleases. We go a journey chiefly to be free of all impediments and of all inconveniences; to leave ourselves behind, much more to get rid of others. It is because I want a little breathing space to muse on indifferent matters, where contemplation

> "May plume her feathers and let grow her wings,
> That in the various bustle of resort
> Were all too ruffled, and sometimes impair'd,"

that I absent myself from the town for awhile, without feeling at a loss the moment I am left by myself. Instead of a friend in a post-chaise or in a Tilbury, to exchange good things with, and vary the same stale topics over again, for once let me have a truce with impertinence. Give me the clear blue sky over my head, and the green turf beneath my feet, a winding road before me, and a three hours' march to dinner—and then to thinking! It is hard if I cannot start some game on these lone heaths. I laugh, I run, I leap, I sing for joy. From the point of yonder rolling cloud, I plunge into my past being, and revel there, as the sun-burnt Indian plunges headlong into the wave that wafts him to his native shore. Then long-forgotten things, like "sunken wrack and sumless treasuries," burst upon my eager sight, and I begin to feel, think, and be myself again. Instead of an awkward silence, broken by attempts at wit or dull common-places, mine is that undisturbed silence of the heart which alone is perfect eloquence. No one likes puns, alliterations, antitheses, argument, and analysis better than I do; but I sometimes had rather be without them. "Leave, oh, leave me to my repose!" I have just now other business in hand, which would seem idle to you, but is with me "very stuff of the conscience." Is not this wild rose sweet without a comment? Does not this daisy leap to my heart set in its coat of emerald? Yet if I were to explain to you the circumstance that has so endeared it to me, you would only smile. Had I not better then keep it to myself, and let it serve me to brood over, from here to yonder craggy point, and from thence onward to the far-distant horizon? I should be but bad company all that way, and therefore prefer being alone. I have heard it said that you may, when the moody fit comes on, walk or ride on yourself, and indulge your reveries. But this looks like a breach of manners, a neglect of others, and you are thinking all the time that you ought to rejoin your party. "Out upon such half-faced fellowship," say I. I like to be either entirely to myself, or entirely at the disposal of others; to talk or be silent, to walk or sit still, to be sociable or solitary. I was pleased with an observation of Mr. Cobbett's, that "he thought it a bad French custom to drink our wine with our meals, and that an Englishman ought to do only one thing at a time." So

I cannot talk and think, or indulge in melancholy musing and lively conversation by fits and starts. "Let me have a companion of my way," says Sterne, "were it but to remark how the shadows lengthen as the sun declines." It is beautifully said: but in my opinion, this continual comparing of notes interferes with the involuntary impression of things upon the mind, and hurts the sentiment. If you only hint what you feel in a kind of dumb show, it is insipid: if you have to explain it, it is making a toil of a pleasure. You cannot read the book of nature, without being perpetually put to the trouble of translating it for the benefit of others. I am for the synthetical method on a journey, in preference to the analytical. I am content to lay in a stock of ideas then, and to examine and anatomise them afterwards. I want to see my vague notions float like the down of the thistle before the breeze, and not to have them entangled in the briars and thorns of controversy. For once, I like to have it all my own way; and this is impossible unless you are alone, or in such company as I do not covet. I have no objection to argue a point with any one for twenty miles of measured road, but not for pleasure. If you remark the scent of a beanfield crossing the road, perhaps your fellow-traveller has no smell. If you point to a distant object, perhaps he is short-sighted, and has to take out his glass to look at it.

There is a feeling in the air, a tone in the colour of a cloud which hits your fancy, but the effect of which you are unable to account for. There is then no sympathy, but an uneasy craving after it, and a dissatisfaction which pursues you on the way, and in the end probably produces ill-humour. Now I never quarrel with myself, and take all my own conclusions for granted till I find it necessary to defend them against objections. It is not merely that you may not be of accord on the objects and circumstances that present themselves before you—these may recall a number of objects, and lead to associations too delicate and refined to be possibly communicated to others. Yet these I love to cherish, and sometimes still fondly clutch them, when I can escape from the throng to do so. To give way to our feelings before company seems extravagance or affectation; and on the other hand, to have to unravel this mystery of our being at every turn, and to make others take an equal interest in it (otherwise the end is not answered) is a task to which few are competent. We must "give it an understanding, but no tongue."

ELIZABETH BARRETT BROWNING
1806–1861

Elizabeth Barrett Browning was celebrated by the reading public of her day for both her poetry and her progressive views on human rights and women's advancement. One of her most famous works is the verse novel *Aurora Leigh* (1856), a narrative which describes a young woman's struggle to fulfil her artistic ambitions in a sexist society. The following extract beautifully captures the young protagonist's sense of euphoria as she roams the gardens of Leigh Hall. The outdoors is the only place where Aurora can be truly childlike in her strict childhood home.

from *Aurora Leigh*

                              I was glad, that day;
The June was in me, with its multitudes
Of nightingales all singing in the dark,
And rosebuds reddening where the calyx split.
I felt so young, so strong, so sure of God!
So glad, I could not choose be very wise!
And, old at twenty, was inclined to pull
My childhood backward in a childish jest
To see the face of 't once more, and farewell!
In which fantastic mood I bounded forth
At early morning,—would not wait so long
As even to snatch my bonnet by the strings,
But, brushing a green trail across the lawn
With my gown in the dew, took will and way
Among the acacias of the shrubberies,
To fly my fancies in the open air
And keep my birthday, till my aunt awoke
To stop good dreams. Meanwhile I murmured on,
As honeyed bees keep humming to themselves,
'The worthiest poets have remained uncrowned
Till death has bleached their foreheads to the bone;
And so with me it must be unless I prove
Unworthy of the grand adversity,
And certainly I would not fail so much.
What, therefore, if I crown myself to-day

In sport, not pride, to learn the feel of it,
Before my brows be numbed as Dante's own
To all the tender pricking of such leaves?
Such leaves! what leaves?'

                    I pulled the branches down
To choose from.

                    'Not the bay! I choose no bay,
(The fates deny us if we are overbold)
Nor myrtle—which means chiefly love; and love
Is something awful which one dares not touch
So early o' mornings. This verbena strains
The point of passionate fragrance; and hard by,
This guelder-rose, at far too slight a beck
Of the wind, will toss about her flower-apples.
Ah—there's my choice,—that ivy on the wall,
That headlong ivy! not a leaf will grow
But thinking of a wreath. Large leaves, smooth leaves,
Serrated like my vines, and half as green.
I like such ivy, bold to leap a height
'Twas strong to climb; as good to grow on graves
As twist about a thyrsus; pretty too,
(And that's not ill) when twisted round a comb.'

Thus speaking to myself, half singing it,
Because some thoughts are fashioned like a bell
To ring with once being touched, I drew a wreath
Drenched, blinding me with dew, across my brow,

And fastening it behind so, turning faced
         My public!—cousin Romney—with a mouth
Twice graver than his eyes.

                    * * *

                    These crowds are very good
For meditation (when we are very strong)
Though love of beauty makes us timorous,
And draws us backward from the coarse town sights
To count the daisies upon dappled fields
And hear the streams bleat on among the hills
In innocent and indolent repose,
While still with silken elegiac thoughts
We wind out from us the distracting world
And die into the chrysalis of a man,
And leave the best that may, to come of us,
In some brown moth. I would be bold and bear
To look into the swarthiest face of things,
For God's sake who has made them.

RABINDRANATH TAGORE
1861–1941

Rabindranath Tagore, sometimes known as the Bard of Bengal, was a writer, poet, musician and a Brahmo Samaj philosopher. A resident of Calcutta, India, he was known for bringing new innovations to Bengali literature and music over the course of his career. In 1913 he was the first Asian to be awarded the Nobel Prize in Literature. In the letters collected in *Glimpses of Bengal* (1921), he describes a journey through the Bengal region along the Padma River by houseboat. In this extract he stops to reflect on the respite he experiences strolling through the countryside, away from the bustle of the city. It is in this wilderness that he finally feels truly free, far removed from any claims on his person.

from *Glimpses of Bengal*

The sky is every now and then overcast and again clears up. Sudden little puffs of wind make the boat lazily creak and groan in all its seams. Thus the day wears on.

It is now past one o'clock. Steeped in this countryside noonday, with its different sounds— the quacking of ducks, the swirl of passing boats, bathers splashing the clothes they wash, the distant shouts from drovers taking cattle across the ford—it is difficult even to imagine the chair-and-table, monotonously dismal routine-life of Calcutta.

Calcutta is as ponderously proper as a Government office. Each of its days comes forth, like coin from a mint, clear-cut and glittering. Ah! those dreary, deadly days, so precisely equal in weight, so decently respectable!

Here I am quit of the demands of my circle, and do not feel like a wound-up machine. Each day is my own. And with leisure and my thoughts I walk the fields, unfettered by bounds of space or time. The evening gradually deepens over earth and sky and water, as with bowed head I stroll along.

THOMAS TRAHERNE
1636/37–1674

Born in Hereford, England, Thomas Traherne was a metaphysical poet, Anglican priest and religious writer. His writings were mostly unknown until they were rediscovered in the early twentieth century. The great themes of his work are the loss of childhood innocence and joy, and with it our ability to commune with God through the natural world. He is often considered to be a forerunner of Romanticism, and has been likened to William Wordsworth, William Blake and Walt Whitman. In the following poem, 'Walking', Traherne expounds upon his favourite theme, encouraging the reader to walk with intentionality, thereby communing with the natural world and the divine.

'Walking'

To walk abroad is, not with Eys,
But Thoughts, the Fields to see and prize;
    Els may the silent Feet,
        Like Logs of Wood,
Mov up and down, and see no Good,
      Nor Joy nor Glory meet.

Ev'n Carts and Wheels their place do change,
But cannot see; tho very strange
    The Glory that is by:
        Dead Puppets may
Mov in the bright and glorious Day,
      Yet not behold the Sky.

And are not Men than they more blind,
Who having Eys yet never find
    The Bliss in which they mov:
        Like Statues dead
They up and down are carried,
      Yet neither see nor lov.

To walk is by a Thought to go;
To mov in Spirit to and fro;
    To mind the Good we see;
        To taste the Sweet;

Observing all the things we meet
     How choice and rich they be.

To note the Beauty of the Day,
And golden Fields of Corn survey;
     Admire each pretty Flow'r
          With its sweet Smell;
To prais their Maker, and to tell
     The Marks of His Great Pow'r.

To fly abroad like activ Bees,
Among the Hedges and the Trees,
     To cull the Dew that lies
          On evry Blade,
From evry Blossom; till we lade
     Our Minds, as they their Thighs.

Observ those rich and glorious things,
The Rivers, Meadows, Woods, and Springs,
     The fructifying Sun;
          To note from far
The Rising of each Twinkling Star
     For us his Race to run.

A little Child these well perceivs,
Who, tumbling in green Grass and Leaves,
     May Rich as Kings be thought,

But there's a Sight
Which perfect Manhood may delight,
    To which we shall be brought.

While in those pleasant Paths we talk
'Tis *that* tow'rds which at last we walk;
        For we may by degrees
            Wisely proceed
Pleasures of Lov and Prais to heed,
        From viewing Herbs and Trees.

DOROTHY WORDSWORTH
1771–1855

Dorothy Wordsworth was a poet, naturalist and diar-
ist whose work was only published after her death.
Her diaries and journals record day-to-day life at
Dove Cottage in Grasmere, often containing her
reflections on long walks she would take with her
brother, William. Other diaries record specific trips,
giving us an insight into the vital connection between
walking and poetry in the Romantic movement. In
the following extract from *Recollections of a Tour
Made in Scotland* (1803), Dorothy describes a warm
encounter with local women walking along Loch
Katrine, and how this moment inspired her brother's
poem 'Stepping Westward'. The poem perfectly captures how going out walking can inspire us and bring
the transcendental into the everyday.

from *Recollections of a Tour Made in Scotland*

We have never had a more delightful walk than this evening. Ben Lomond and the three pointed-topped mountains of Loch Lomond, which we had seen from the Garrison, were very majestic under the clear sky, the lake perfectly calm, the air sweet and mild. I felt that it was much more interesting to visit a place where we have been before than it can possibly be the first time, except under peculiar circumstances. The sun had been set for some time, when, being within a quarter of a mile of the ferryman's hut, our path having led us close to the shore of the calm lake, we met two neatly dressed women, without hats, who had probably been taking their Sunday evening's walk. One of them said to us in a friendly, soft tone of voice, 'What! you are stepping westward?' I cannot describe how affecting this simple expression was in that remote place, with the western sky in front, yet glowing with the departed sun. William wrote the following poem long after, in remembrance of his feelings and mine:—

> 'What! you are stepping westward?' Yea,
> 'Twould be a wildish destiny
> If we, who thus together roam

In a strange land, and far from home,
Were in this place the guests of chance:
Yet who would stop, or fear to advance,
Though home or shelter he had none,
With such a sky to lead him on?

The dewy ground was dark and cold,
Behind all gloomy to behold,
And stepping westward seem'd to be
A kind of heavenly destiny;
I liked the greeting, 'twas a sound
Of something without place or bound;
And seem'd to give me spiritual right
To travel through that region bright.

The voice was soft; and she who spake
Was walking by her native Lake;
The salutation was to me
The very sound of courtesy;
Its power was felt, and while my eye
Was fix'd upon the glowing sky,
The echo of the voice enwrought
A human sweetness with the thought
Of travelling through the world that lay
Before me in my endless way.

JESSIE REDMON FAUSET
1882–1961

Jessie Redmon Fauset was a novelist, poet and essayist who was also the literary editor of *The Crisis*, the magazine of the civil rights organization NAACP. Her position as editor made her an important champion of emerging voices in the Harlem Renaissance. Her literary work shaped African American literature, and her poem 'Rondeau', first published in *The Crisis* in 1912, celebrates abandoning cerebral work for the heady enjoyment of roaming the outdoor world.

'Rondeau'

When April's here and meadows wide
Once more with spring's sweet growths are pied,
    I close each book, drop each pursuit,
    And past the brook, no longer mute,
I joyous roam the countryside.

Look, here the violets shy abide
And there the mating robins hide—
      How keen my senses, how acute,
        When April's here!

And list! down where the shimmering tide
Hard by that farthest hill doth glide,
     Rise faint strains from shepherd's flute,
     Pan's pipes and Berecyntian lute.
Each sight, each sound fresh joys provide
        When April's here.

ANN RADCLIFFE
1764–1823

Ann Radcliffe was an English novelist who pioneered the Gothic genre. Wildly popular in her day with critics and the public alike, she was known for giving rational explanations for things initially deemed to be supernatural. In this following extract from *The Mysteries of Udolpho* (1794), Emily St. Aubert encounters the first of many mysteries and strange occurrences in the narrative: an unsigned love poem. At this point in *Udolpho*, walking is Emily's retreat from life into an Eden-like bliss, her means of everyday adventure. However, as the story takes Emily through the Pyrenees and down to the Mediterranean, she understands the latent risk in exploration: that the walker can easily stumble into places that are terrifying, or even supernatural.

from *The Mysteries of Udolpho*

It was one of Emily's earliest pleasures to ramble among the scenes of nature; nor was it in the soft and glowing landscape that she most delighted; she loved more the wild wood walks, that skirted the mountain; and still more the mountain's stupendous recesses, where the silence and grandeur of solitude impressed a sacred awe upon her heart, and lifted her thoughts to the GOD OF HEAVEN AND EARTH. In scenes like these she would often linger alone, wrapt in a melancholy charm, till the last gleam of day faded from the west; till the lonely sound of a sheep-bell, or the distant bark of a watch-dog, were all that broke on the stillness of the evening. Then, the gloom of the woods; the trembling of their leaves, at intervals, in the breeze; the bat, flitting on the twilight; the cottage lights, now seen, and now lost—were circumstances that awakened her mind into effort, and led to enthusiasm and poetry.

Her favourite walk was to a little fishing house, belonging to St. Aubert, in a woody glen, on the margin of a rivulet that descended to the Pyrenees, and, after foaming among their rocks, wound its silent way beneath the shades it reflected. Above the woods, that screened this glen, rose the lofty summits of the Pyrenees, which often burst boldly on the eye, through the glades below. Sometimes the shattered face of a rock only was seen, crowned with wild shrubs; or a shepherd's cabin seated on a cliff, overshadowed by dark cypress, or waving ash. Emerging from the deep recesses of the woods, the glade opened to the distant landscape, where the rich pastures and vine-covered slopes of Gascony gradually declined to the plains, and there, on the winding shores of the Garonne, groves, and hamlets, and villas—their outlines softened by distance—melted from the eye into one rich harmonious tint.

This, too, was the favourite retreat of St. Aubert, to which he frequently withdrew from the fervour of noon, with his wife, his daughter, and his books; or came at the sweet evening hour to welcome the silent dusk, or to listen to the music of the nightingale. Sometimes, too, he brought music of his own, and awakened every fair echo with the tender accents of his oboe; and often have the tones of Emily's voice drawn sweetness from the waves, over which they trembled.

It was in one of her excursions to this spot, that she observed the following lines written with a pencil on a part of the wainscot:

SONNET

Go, pencil! faithful to thy master's sighs,
  Go—tell the Goddess of this fairy scene,
  When next her light steps wind these wood-walks
    green,
Whence all his tears, his tender sorrows, rise;

Ah! paint her form, her soul-illumin'd eyes,
  The sweet expression of her pensive face,
  The light'ning smile, the animated grace—
The portrait well the lover's voice supplies;

Speaks all his heart must feel, his tongue would say,
  Yet ah! not all his heart must sadly feel!
  How oft the flow'ret's silken leaves conceal
The drug that steals the vital spark away!

And who that gazes on that angel-smile,
Would fear its charm, or think it could beguile!

These lines were not inscribed to any person:
Emily therefore could not apply them to herself,
though she was undoubtedly the nymph of these
shades. Having glanced round the little circle of her
acquaintance without being detained by a suspicion
as to whom they could be addressed, she was com-
pelled to rest in uncertainty; an uncertainty which

would have been more painful to an idle mind than it was to hers. She had no leisure to suffer this circumstance, trifling at first, to swell into importance by frequent remembrance. The little vanity it had excited (for the incertitude which forbade her to presume upon having inspired the sonnet, forbade her also to disbelieve it) passed away, and the incident was dismissed from her thoughts amid her books, her studies, and the exercise of social charities.

FRANCES BURNEY
1752–1840

Fanny Burney was an English novelist, playwright and woman of letters whose novel *Evelina* (1778) is considered a milestone in the evolution of the 'novel of manners'. Her final novel, *The Wanderer; or, Female Difficulties* (1814) took fourteen years to write and explores the hardships that surround the pursuit of financial or social independence as a Victorian woman. The mysterious wandering protagonist is trying to make her way in the world while remaining anonymous. Constant movement helps her hold on to her independence, although her lifestyle is often met with disbelief.

from *The Wanderer*

CHAPTER VII

The house of Mrs. Maple was just without the town
of Lewes, and the Wanderer, upon her arrival there,
learnt that Brighthelmstone was still eight miles farther. She earnestly desired to go on immediately;
but how undertake such a journey on foot, so late,
and in the dark month of December, when the
night appears to commence at four o'clock in the
afternoon? Her travelling companions both left her
in the court-yard, and she was fain, uninvited, to
follow them to the apartment of the housekeeper;
where she was beginning an apology upon the
necessity that urged her intrusion, when Selina came
skipping into the room.

The stranger, conceiving some hope of assistance
from her extreme youth, and air of good humour,
besought her interest with Mrs. Maple for permis-
sion to remain in the house till the next day. Selina
carried the request with alacrity, and, almost instantly returning, gave orders to the housekeeper to
prepare a bed for her fellow-traveller, in the little
room upon the stairs.

The gratitude excited by this support was so
pleasant to the young patronness, that she accompanied her *protegée* to the destined little apartment,

superintended all the regulations for her accommodation and refreshments, and took so warm a fancy to her, that she made her a visit every other half-hour in the course of the evening; during which she related, with earnest injunctions to secresy, all the little incidents of her little life, finishing her narration by intimating, in a rapturous whisper, that she should very soon have a house of her own, in which her aunt Maple would have no sort of authority. "And then," added she, nodding, "perhaps I may ask you to come and see me!"

No one else appeared; and the stranger might tranquilly have passed the night, but from internal disturbance how she should reach Brighthelmstone the following morning, without carriage, friends, money, or knowledge of the road thither.

Before the tardy light invited her to rise the next day, her new young friend came flying into the room. "I could not sleep," she cried, "all last night, for the thought of a play that I am to have a very pretty dress for; and that we have fixed upon acting amongst ourselves; and so I got up on purpose to tell you of it, for fear you should be gone."

She then read through every word of her own part, without a syllable of any other.

They were both soon afterwards sent for into the parlour by Elinor, who was waiting breakfast for

Mrs. Maple, with Harleigh and Ireton. "My dear demoiselle," she cried, "how fares it? We were all so engrossed last night, about a comedy that we have been settling to massacre, that I protest I quite forgot you."

"I ought only, Madam," answered the stranger, with a sigh, "to wonder, and to be grateful that you have ever thought of me."

"Why what's the matter with you now? Why are you so solemn? Is your noble courage cast down? What are you projecting? What's your plan?"

"When I have been to Brighthelmstone, Madam, when I have seen who—or what may await me there—"

Mrs. Maple, now appearing, angrily demanded who had invited her into the parlour? telling her to repair to the kitchen, and make known what she wanted through some of the servants.

The blood mounted into the cheeks of the Incognita, but she answered only by a distant courtsie, and turning to Elinor and Selina, besought them to accept her acknowledgements for their goodness, and retired.

Selina and Elinor, following her into the anteroom, asked how she meant to travel?

She had one way only in her power; she must walk.

"Walk?" exclaimed Harleigh, joining them, "in such a season? And by such roads?"

"Walk?" cried Ireton, advancing also, "eight miles? In December?"

"And why not, gentlemen?" called out Mrs. Maple, "How would you have such a body as that go, if she must not walk? What else has she got her feet for?"

"Are you sure," said Ireton, "that you know the way?"

"I was never in this part of the world till now."

"Ha! Ha! pleasant enough! And what are you to do about money? Did you ever find that purse of yours that you—lost, I think, at Dover?"

"Never!"

"Better and better!" cried Ireton, laughing again, yet feeling for his own purse, and sauntering towards the hall.

Harleigh was already out of sight.

"Poor soul!" said Selina, "I am sure, for one, I'll help her."

"Let us make a subscription," said Elinor, producing half a guinea, and looking round to Mrs. Maple.

Selina joined the same sum, full of glee to give, for the first time, as much as her sister.

Mrs. Maple clamorously ordered them to shut the parlour door.

With shame, yet joy, the stranger accepted the two half guineas, intimated her hopes that she should soon repay them, repeated her thanks, and took leave.

WILLIAM COWPER
1731–1800

William Cowper (pronounced Cooper), was one of the most popular poets of his day, now primarily remembered for his hymns. His poetry was considered distinctive and innovative at the time because of its lifelike depictions of rural life. Walking to facilitate meditation is an important theme in the following extract from 'The Winter Walk at Noon', taken from his long poem *The Task* (1785). It describes the joy of wallowing in the emotions that are stirred up by the sights and sounds of the rural landscape, or as Cowper pithily puts it, walking is a time when 'the heart / May give a useful lesson to the head'.

from 'The Winter Walk at Noon'

The night was winter in his roughest mood,
The morning sharp and clear; but now at noon
Upon the southern side of the slant hills,
And where the woods fence off the northern blast,
The season smiles, resigning all its rage,
And has the warmth of May. The vault is blue
Without a cloud, and white without a speck
The dazzling splendour of the scene below.
Again the harmony comes o'er the vale,
And through the trees I view th'embattled tow'r
Whence all the music. I again perceive
The soothing influence of the wafted strains,
And settle in soft musings, as I tread
The walk still verdant under oaks and elms,
Whose outspread branches overarch the glade.
The roof, though movable through all its length,
As the wind sways it, has yet well sufficed,
And, intercepting in their silent fall
The frequent flakes, has kept a path for me.
No noise is here, or none that hinders thought.
The redbreast warbles still, but is content
With slender notes and more than half suppressed.
Pleased with his solitude, and flitting light
From spray to spray, where'er he rests he shakes
From many a twig the pendent drops of ice,

That tinkle in the withered leaves below.
Stillness, accompanied with sounds so soft,
Charms more than silence. Meditation here
May think down hours to moments. Here the heart
May give a useful lesson to the head,
And learning wiser grow without his books.

★ ★ ★

Here unmolested, through whatever sign
The sun proceeds, I wander; neither mist,
Nor freezing sky, nor sultry, checking me,
Nor stranger intermeddling with my joy.
Ev'n in the spring and playtime of the year
That calls the unwonted villager abroad
With all her little ones, a sportive train,
To gather king-cups in the yellow mead,
And prank their hair with daisies, or to pick
A cheap but wholesome salad from the brook,
These shades are all my own. The tim'rous hare,
Grown so familiar with her frequent guest,
Scarce shuns me; and the stock-dove unalarmed
Sits cooing in the pine-tree, nor suspends
His long love-ditty for my near approach.
Drawn from his refuge in some lonely elm
That age or injury has hollowed deep,
Where on his bed of wool and matted leaves
He has outslept the winter, ventures forth

To frisk awhile, and bask in the warm sun,
The squirrel, flippant, pert, and full of play.
He sees me, and at once, swift as a bird,
Ascends the neighb'ring beech; there whisks his brush,
And perks his ears, and stamps and scolds aloud,
With all the prettiness of feigned alarm,
And anger insignificantly fierce.

The heart is hard in nature, and unfit
For human fellowship, as being void
Of sympathy, and therefore dead alike
To love and friendship both, that is not pleased
With sight of animals enjoying life,
Nor feels their happiness augment his own.
The bounding fawn that darts across the glade
When none pursues, through mere delight of heart,
And spirits buoyant with excess of glee;
The horse, as wanton and almost as fleet,
That skims the spacious meadow at full speed,
Then stops and snorts, and throwing high his heels,
Starts to the voluntary race again;
The very kine that gambol at high noon,
The total herd receiving first from one,
That leads the dance, a summons to be gay,
Though wild their strange vagaries, and uncouth
Their efforts, yet resolved with one consent
To give such act and utt'rance as they may

To ecstasy too big to be suppressed—
These, and a thousand images of bliss,
With which kind Nature graces ev'ry scene
Where cruel man defeats not her design,
Impart to the benevolent, who wish
All that are capable of pleasure pleased,
A far superior happiness to theirs,
The comfort of a reasonable joy.

🌿

ROBERT SOUTHEY
1774–1843

Robert Southey was the English Poet Laureate from
1813 until 1843. He is considered part of the Romantic school and one of the lesser-known Lake Poets.
He was also a man of letters, an essayist, biographer
and novelist. In 1807 he published an epistolary
novel, *Letters from England*, under the pseudonym of
fictional Spanish tourist Don Manuel Alvarez Espriella. The narrative gives an account of a journey
made through England, which becomes a vehicle for
Southey to offer his views on various social problems
through a supposed 'outsider's perspective'. The following passage comes from Don Alvarez Espriella's
stay in London, where he reports on the perils of city
pedestrianism during rush hour, presenting us with a
vision of walking that is wildly different from the
kind that we typically associate with the Romantics.
The city walker has little head space for meditation,
bombarded with exciting sights and sounds and
bodies.

from *Letters from England*

The nearer we drew the greater was the throng. It was a sight truly surprising to behold all the inhabitants of this immense city walking abroad at midnight, and distinctly seen by the light of ten thousand candles. This was particularly striking in Oxford Street, which is nearly half a league in length;—as far as the eye could reach either way the parallel lines of light were seen narrowing towards each other. Here, however, we could still advance without difficulty, and the carriages rattled along unobstructed. But in the immediate vicinity of Portman Square it was very different. Never before had I beheld such multitudes assembled. The middle of the street was completely filled with coaches, so immoveably locked together, that many persons who wished to cross passed under the horses' bellies without fear, and without danger. The unfortunate persons within had no such means of escape; they had no possible way of extricating themselves, unless they could crawl out of the window of one coach into the window of another; there was no room to open a door. There they were, and there they must remain, patiently or impatiently; and there in fact they did remain the greater part of the night, till the lights were burnt out, and the crowd clearing away left them at liberty.

We who were on foot had better fortune, but we laboured hard for it. There were two ranks of people, one returning from the square, the other pressing on to it. Exertion was quite needless; man was wedged to man, he who was behind you pressed you against him who was before; I had nothing to do but to work out elbow room that I might not be squeezed to death, and to float on with the tide. But this tide was frequently at a stop; some obstacle at the further end of the street checked it, and still the crowd behind was increasing in depth. We tried the first entrance to the square in vain; it was utterly impossible to get in, and finding this we crossed into the counter current, and were carried out by the stream. A second and a third entrance we tried with no better fortune; at the fourth, the only remaining avenue, we were more successful. To this, which is at the outskirts of the town, there was one way inaccessible by carriages, and it was not crowded by walkers, because the road was bad, there were no lamps, and the way was not known. By this route, however, we entered the avenue immediately opposite to M. Otto's, and raising ourselves by the help of a garden-wall, overlooked the crowd, and thus obtained a full and uninterrupted sight, of what thousands and tens of thousands were vainly struggling to see. To describe it, splendid as it was, is impossible; the whole building presented a front of light.

CHARLES DICKENS
1812–1870

Charles Dickens is considered to be the great Victorian novelist. A social reformer as well as an author, his work is often concerned with the city, sketching a detailed picture of Victorian disease, suffering and want. In the following extract from his personal essay 'Night Walks' (1860), Dickens, suffering from insomnia, puts himself in the shoes of a homeless person. As he walks the streets of London at night he begins to understand how walking can be a coping mechanism. Lonely, cold and out of doors while the rest of the city sleeps, the homeless walk the streets in search of comfort and company.

from 'Night Walks'

CHAPTER XIII

Some years ago, a temporary inability to sleep, referable to a distressing impression, caused me to walk about the streets all night, for a series of several nights. The disorder might have taken a long time to conquer, if it had been faintly experimented on in bed; but, it was soon defeated by the brisk treatment of getting up directly after lying down, and going out, and coming home tired at sunrise.

In the course of those nights, I finished my education in a fair amateur experience of houselessness. My principal object being to get through the night, the pursuit of it brought me into sympathetic relations with people who have no other object every night in the year.

The month was March, and the weather damp, cloudy, and cold. The sun not rising before half-past five, the night perspective looked sufficiently long at half-past twelve: which was about my time for confronting it.

The restlessness of a great city, and the way in which it tumbles and tosses before it can get to sleep, formed one of the first entertainments offered to the contemplation of us houseless people. I lasted about two hours. We lost a great deal o companionship when the late public-houses turned their lamps out, and when the potmen thrust the last brawling drunkards into the street; but stray vehicles and stray people were left us, after that. If we were very lucky, a policeman's rattle sprang and a fray turned up; but, in general, surprisingly little of this diversion was provided. Except in the Haymarket, which is the worst kept part of London, and about Kent Street in the Borough, and along a portion of the line of the Old Kent Road, the peace was seldom violently broken. But, it was always the case that London, as if in imitation of individual citizens belonging to it, had expiring fits and starts of restlessness. After all seemed quiet, if one cab rattled by, half a dozen would surely follow; and Houselessness even observed that intoxicated people appeared to be magnetically attracted towards each other; so that we knew when we saw one drunken object staggering against the shutters of a shop, that another drunken object would stagger up before five minutes were out, to fraternise or fight with it. When we made a divergence from the regular species of drunkard, the thin-armed puff-faced leaden-lipped gin-drinker, and encountered a rarer specimen of a more decent appearance, fifty to one but that specimen was dressed in soiled mourning. As the street experience in the night, so the street experience in the day; the common folk who come unexpectedly into a little property, come unexpectedly into a deal of liquor.

At length these flickering sparks would die away, worn out—the last veritable sparks of waking life trailed from some late pieman or hot potato man—and London would sink to rest. And then the yearning of the houseless mind would be for any sign of company, any lighted place, any movement, anything suggestive of any one being up—nay, even so much as awake, for the houseless eye looked out for lights in windows.

Walking the streets under the pattering rain, Houselessness would walk and walk and walk, seeing nothing but the interminable tangle of streets, save at a corner, here and there, two policemen in conversation, or the sergeant or inspector looking after his men. Now and then in the night—but rarely—Houselessness would become aware of a furtive head peering out of a doorway a few yards before him, and, coming up with the head, would find a man standing bolt upright to keep within the doorway's shadow, and evidently intent upon no particular service to society. Under a kind of fascination, and in a ghostly silence suitable to the time, Houselessness and this gentleman would eye one another from head to foot, and so, without exchange of speech, part, mutually suspicious. Drip, drip, drip, from ledge and coping, splash from pipes and water-spouts, and by-and-by the houseless shadow would fall upon the stones that pave the way to Waterloo Bridge; it being in the houseless mind to have a halfpenny worth of excuse for saying "Good night" to the toll-keeper, and catching a glimpse of his fire. A good fire and a good great-coat and a good woollen neck-shawl, were comfortable things to see in conjunction with the toll-keeper; also his brisk wakefulness was excellent company when he rattled the change of halfpence down upon that metal table of his, like a man who defied the night, with all its sorrowful thoughts, and didn't care for the coming of dawn.

CHARLOTTE LENNOX
1730–1804

Charlotte Lennox was a Scottish writer born in
Gibraltar. After a brief and unsuccessful career as an
actress she turned to poetry and prose, and was
quickly ushered into the London literary scene by
the likes of Samuel Johnson. Her most famous
novel, which remained anonymous until her death,
The Female Quixote (1752), parodies the tradition of
Miguel de Cervantes's *Don Quixote* (1605, 1615). The
protagonist Arabella is an avid reader who believes
that real life is exactly like her beloved French
romance novels. Unable to distinguish between literature and real life, she behaves and speaks like a
romantic heroine. In Arabella's mind, a simple walk
through London puts her at risk of attack. In this
extract, her fantastic imaginings prompt her to
throw herself into the River Thames as means of
escape, in the manner of the mythical Clelia, who
threw herself into the River Tiber.

from *The Female Quixote*

Our fair and afflicted Heroine, accompanied by the
Ladies we have mention'd, having cross'd the River,
pursu'd their Walk upon its winding Banks, enter-
taining themselves with the usual Topicks of Conversation among young Ladies, such as their Winnings
and Losings at *Brag*, the Prices of Silks, the newest
Fashions, the best Hair-Cutter, the Scandal at the
last Assembly, &c.

Arabella was so disgusted with this (as she
thought) insipid Discourse, which gave no Relief
to the Anxiety of her Mind, but added a Kind of
Fretfulness and Impatience to her Grief, that she
resolv'd to quit them, and with Lucy, go in quest of
the Princess of Gaul's Retreat.

The Ladies, however, insisted upon her not leaving them; and her Excuse that she was going in
search of an unfortunate Unknown, for whom she
had vow'd a Friendship, made them all immediately
resolve to accompany her, extremely diverted with
the Oddity of the Design, and sacrificing her to their
Mirth by sly Leers, Whispers, stifled Laughs, and a

thousand little sprightly Sallies, which the disconsolate Arabella took no Notice of, so deeply were her Thoughts engag'd.

Tho' she knew not which Way to direct her Steps, yet concluding the melancholy Cynecia would certainly chuse some very solitary Place for her Residence, she rambled about among the least frequented Paths, follow'd by the young Ladies, who ardently desir'd to see this unfortunate unknown; tho' at Arabella's earnest Request, they promis'd not to shew themselves to the Lady, who, she inform'd them, for very urgent Reasons, was oblig'd to keep herself conceal'd.

Fatiguing as this Ramble was to the delicate Spirits of Arabella's Companions, they were enabled to support it by the Diversion her Behaviour afforded them.

Every Peasant she met, she enquir'd if a Beautiful Lady disguis'd did not dwell somewhere there about.

To some she gave a Description of her Person, to others an Account of the Domesticks that were with her; not forgetting her Dress, her Melancholy, and the great Care she took to keep herself conceal'd.

These strange Enquiries, with the strange Language in which they were made, not a little surpriz'd the good People to whom she address'd herself, ye

96

mov'd to Respect by the majestick Loveliness of her Person, they answer'd her in the Negative, without any Mixture of Scoff and Impertinence.

How unfavourable is Chance, said Arabella fretting at the Disappointment, to Persons who have any Reliance upon it! This Lady that I have been in Search of so long without Success, may probably be found by others who do not seek her, whose Presence she may wish to avoid, yet not be able.

The young Ladies finding it grew late, express'd their Apprehensions at being without any Attendants; and desir'd Arabella to give over her Search for that Day. Arabella at this Hint of Danger, enquir'd very earnestly, If they apprehended any Attempts to carry them away? And without staying for an Answer, urg'd them to walk Home as fast as possible, apologizing for the Danger into which she had so indiscreetly drawn both them and herself; yet added her Hopes, that, if any Attempt should be made upon their Liberty, some generous Cavalier would pass by who would rescue them: A Thing so common, that they had no Reason to despair of it.

Arabella construing the Silence with which her Companions heard these Assurances, into a Doubt of their being so favoured by Fortune, proceeded to inform them of several Instances wherein Ladies

97

met with unexpected Relief and Deliverance from Ravishers.

She mentioned particularly the Rescue of Statira by her own Brother, whom she imagin'd for many Years dead; that of the Princess Berenice by an absolute Stranger, and many others, whose Names, Characters and Adventures she occasionally ran over; all which the young Ladies heard with inconceivable Astonishment. And the Detail had such an Effect upon Arabella's Imagination, bewilder'd as it was in the Follies of Romances, that 'spying three or four Horsemen riding along the Road towards them, she immediately concluded they would be all seiz'd and carried off.

Posses'd with this Belief, she utter'd a loud Cry and flew to the Water-side, which alarming the Ladies, who could not imagine what was the Matter they ran after her as fast as possible.

Arabella stop'd when she came to the Water-side and looking round about, and not perceiving any Boat to waft them over to Richmond, a Thought suddenly darted into her Mind, worthy those ingenious Books which gave it Birth.

Turning therefore to the Ladies, who all at once were enquiring the Cause of her Fright:

'Tis now, my fair Companions, said she, with solemn Accent, that the Destinies have furnish'd you with an Opportunity of displaying in a Manner truly Heroick, the Sublimity of your Virtue, and the Grandeur of your Courage to the World.

The Action we have it in our Power to perform will immortalize our Fame, and raise us to a Pitch of Glory equal to that of the renown'd Clelia herself.

Like her, we may expect Statues erected to our Honour; like her, be propos'd as Patterns to Heroines in ensuing Ages; and like her, perhaps, meet with Sceptres and Crowns for our Reward.

What that beauteous Roman Lady perform'd to preserve herself from Violation by the impious Sextus, let us imitate to avoid the Violence our intended Ravishers yonder come to offer us.

Fortune, which has thrown us into this Exigence, presents us the Means of gloriously escaping: And the Admiration and Esteem of all Ages to come, will be the Recompence of our noble Daring.

Once more, my fair Companions, if your Honour be dear to you, if an immortal Glory be worth your seeking, follow the Example I shall set you, and equal with me the Roman Clelia.

Saying this, she plung'd into the Thames, intending to swim over it, as Clelia did the Tyber.

The young Ladies, who had listened with silent astonishment at the long Speech she had made

99

them, the Purport of which not one of them understood, scream'd out aloud at this horrid Spectacle, and wringing their Hands, ran backwards and forwards like distracted Persons, crying for Help. Lucy tore her Hair, and was in the utmost Agony of Grief, when Mr. Roberts, who, as we have said before, kept them always in Sight, having observ'd Arabella running towards the Water-side, follow'd them as fast as he could, and came Time enough up to see her frantick Action. Jumping into the River immediately after her, he caught hold of her Gown, and drew her after him to the Shore. A Boat that Instant appearing, he put her into it, senseless, and to all Appearance dead. He and Lucy supporting her, they were wafted over in a few Moments to the other Side; her House being near the River, Mr. Roberts carry'd her in his Arms to it; and as soon as he saw her shew Signs of returning Life, left her to the Care of the Women, who made haste to put her into a warm Bed, and ran to find out Mr. Glanville, as we have related.

JEAN-JACQUES ROUSSEAU
1712–1778

The Genevan philosopher and writer Jean-Jacques Rousseau was a key thinker in the European Enlightenment period. His writings influenced the French Revolution and he is often called the Father of Romanticism, because of the generation of poets that he inspired. One of his defining ideas, as first set out in *Discourse on the Arts and Sciences*, is that the march of human civilization has had a damaging effect on human nature and morality. He argued that 'progress' has brought humankind away from *l'état de nature*, the state of nature, and corrupted the human race with self-love. In the following extract from his autobiography, Rousseau reflects on hiking in his youth, claiming that this was when he felt most alive.

from *The Confessions*
of Jean-Jacques Rousseau

What I most regret is not having kept a journal of
my travels, being conscious that a number of interesting details have slipped my memory; for never did
I exist so completely, never live so thoroughly, never
was so much myself, if I may dare to use the expression, as in those journeys made on foot. Walking
animates and enlivens my spirits; I can hardly think
when in a state of inactivity; my body must be exercised to make my judgment active. The view of a fine
country, a succession of agreeable prospects, a free
air, a good appetite, and the health I gain by walking; the freedom of inns, and the distance from
everything that can make me recollect the depend-
ence of my situation, conspire to free my soul, and
give boldness to my thoughts, throwing me, in a
manner, into the immensity of beings, where I com-
bine, choose, and appropriate them to my fancy
without constraint or fear. I dispose of all nature as
I please; my heart wandering from object to object
approximates and unites with those that please it
is surrounded by charming images, and becomes
intoxicated with delicious sensations. If, attempting
to render these permanent, I am amused in describ-
ing them to myself what glow of colouring, what

energy of expression, do I give them! It has been said that all these are to be found in my works, though written in the decline of life. Oh! had those of my early youth been seen, those made during my travels, composed, but never written! Why did I not write them? will be asked. And why should I have written them? I may answer. Why deprive myself of the actual charm of my enjoyments to inform others what I enjoyed? What to me were readers, the public, or all the world, while I was mounting the empyrean? Besides, did I carry pens, paper, and ink with me? Had I recollected all these, not a thought would have occurred worth preserving. I do not foresee when I shall have ideas; they come when they please, and not when I call for them; either they avoid me altogether, or, rushing in crowds, overwhelm me with their force and number. Ten volumes a day would not suffice barely to enumerate my thoughts; how then should I find time to write them? In stopping, I thought of nothing but a hearty dinner; on departing, of nothing but a charming walk; I felt that a new paradise awaited me at the door, and eagerly leaped forward to enjoy it.

WILLIAM WORDSWORTH
1770–1850

One of the most famous names in English poetry and a leading figure in the Romantic movement, William Wordsworth had a great love of walking. His friend Thomas de Quincey estimated that Wordsworth must have covered around 175,000 miles on foot over the course of his life. For Wordsworth, walking was a part of the creative process – he would often compose as he walked, so it's no surprise that walking often became the subject of his work. His poems reveal that walking was a cornerstone of his existence, more of a lifestyle than an occasional leisure activity. In the following poems, Wordsworth describes the breadth of walking: how it can provoke both lofty thoughts and childlike contentment, how it can take us into our heads or bring us fully into our bodily senses.

'How sweet it is, when mother Fancy rocks'

How sweet it is, when mother Fancy rocks
The wayward brain, to saunter through a wood!
An old place, full of many a lovely brood,
Tall trees, green arbours, and ground flowers in flocks;
And Wild rose tip-toe upon hawthorn stocks,
Like to a bonny Lass, who plays her pranks
At Wakes and Fairs with wandering Mountebanks,
When she stands cresting the Clown's head, and mocks
The crowd beneath her. Verily I think,
Such place to me is sometimes like a dream
Or map of the whole world: thoughts, link by link
Enter through ears and eyesight, with such gleam
Of all things, that at last in fear I shrink,
And leap at once from the delicious stream.

'Written in very early Youth'

Calm is all nature as a resting wheel.
The Kine are couch'd upon the dewy grass;
The Horse alone, seen dimly as I pass,
Is up, and cropping yet his later meal:
Dark is the ground; a slumber seems to steal
O'er vale, and mountain, and the starless sky.
Now, in this blank of things, a harmony,
Home-felt, and home-created, seems to heal
That grief for which the senses still supply
Fresh food; for only then, when memory
Is hush'd, am I at rest. My Friends, restrain
Those busy cares that would allay my pain:
Oh! leave me to myself; nor let me feel
The officious touch that makes me droop again.

'It is a beauteous Evening, calm and free'

It is a beauteous Evening, calm and free;
The holy time is quiet as a Nun
Breathless with adoration; the broad sun
Is sinking down in its tranquillity;
The gentleness of heaven is on the Sea:
Listen! the mighty Being is awake
And doth with his eternal motion make
A sound like thunder—everlastingly.
Dear Child! dear Girl! that walkest with me here,
If thou appear'st untouch'd by solemn thought,
Thy nature is not therefore less divine:
Thou liest in Abraham's bosom all the year;
And worshipp'st at the Temple's inner shrine,
God being with thee when we know it not.

'I wandered lonely as a Cloud'

I wandered lonely as a Cloud
That floats on high o'er Vales and Hills,
When all at once I saw a crowd,
A host, of dancing Daffodils;
Along the Lake, beneath the trees,
Ten thousand dancing in the breeze.

The waves beside them danced, but they
Outdid the sparkling waves in glee:—
A Poet could not but be gay
In such a laughing company:
I gaz'd—and gaz'd—but little thought
What wealth the shew to me had brought:

For oft when on my couch I lie
In vacant or in pensive mood,
They flash upon that inward eye
Which is the bliss of solitude,
And then my heart with pleasure fills,
And dances with the Daffodils.

ALFRED TENNYSON
1809–1892

Alfred Tennyson was considered to be the mouth-piece of Queen Victoria's reign, serving as Poet Laureate of Great Britain and Ireland between 1850 and 1892. The popularity which he enjoyed in his own lifetime has continued to the present day. The following extracts are from his poem 'In Memoriam A. H. H.' (1850), which was written as a eulogy for his best friend Arthur Hallam, who died suddenly at only twenty-two years old. The poem is really about the journey of grief; in fact, it was originally meant to be titled 'The Way of the Soul'. Alongside the central emotional journey, journeys on foot play an important role. Walking provides the narrator with a language for grief; before Arthur's death, their friendship was like a companionable walk, but now the narrator walks the path alone. Furthermore, walking about his university town becomes a means of time travel, as physical spaces evoke memory, a bittersweet experience where things are 'the same, but not the same'.

from 'In Memoriam A. H. H.'

XXII

The path by which we twain did go,
    Which led by tracts that pleased us well,
    Thro' four sweet years arose and fell,
From flower to flower, from snow to snow:

And we with singing cheer'd the way,
    And, crown'd with all the season lent,
    From April on to April went,
And glad at heart from May to May:

But where the path we walk'd began
    To slant the fifth autumnal slope,
    As we descended following Hope,
There sat the Shadow fear'd of man;

Who broke our fair companionship,
    And spread his mantle dark and cold;
    And wrapt thee formless in the fold,
And dull'd the murmur on thy lip;

And bore thee where I could not see
    Nor follow, tho' I walk in haste;
    And think, that somewhere in the waste
The Shadow sits and waits for me.

XXIII

Now, sometimes in my sorrow shut,
    Or breaking into song by fits;
    Alone, alone, to where he sits,
The Shadow cloak'd from head to foot,

Who keeps the keys of all the creeds,
    I wander, often falling lame,
    And looking back to whence I came,
Or on to where the pathway leads;

And crying, How changed from where it ran
    Thro' lands where not a leaf was dumb;
    But all the lavish hills would hum
The murmur of a happy Pan:

When each by turns was guide to each,
    And Fancy light from Fancy caught,
    And Thought leapt out to wed with Thought,
Ere Thought could wed itself with Speech;

And all we met was fair and good,
    And all was good that Time could bring,
    And all the secret of the Spring
Moved in the chambers of the blood;

And many an old philosophy
    On Argive heights divinely sang,
    And round us all the thicket rang
To many a flute of Arcady.

LXXXVI

I past beside the reverend walls
    In which of old I wore the gown;
    I roved at random thro' the town,
And saw the tumult of the halls;

And heard once more in college fanes
    The storm their high-built organs make,
    And thunder-music, rolling, shake
The prophet blazon'd on the panes;

And caught once more the distant shout,
    The measured pulse of racing oars
    Among the willows; paced the shores
And many a bridge, and all about

The same gray flats again, and felt
    The same, but not the same; and last
    Up that long walk of limes I past
To see the rooms in which he dwelt.

Another name was on the door:
>   I linger'd; all within was noise
>   Of songs, and clapping hands, and boys
That crash'd the glass and beat the floor;

Where once we held debate, a band
>   Of youthful friends, on mind and art,
>   And labour, and the changing mart,
And all the framework of the land;

When one would aim an arrow fair,
>   But send it slackly from the string;
>   And one would pierce an outer ring,
And one an inner, here and there;

And last the master-bowman, he
>   Would cleave the mark. A willing ear
>   We lent him. Who, but hung to hear
The rapt oration flowing free

From point to point, with power and grace
>   And music in the bounds of law,
>   To those conclusions when we saw
The God within him light his face,

And seem to lift the form, and glow
    In azure orbits heavenly-wise;
    And over those ethereal eyes
The bar of Michael Angelo.

C

We leave the well-beloved place
    Where first we gazed upon the sky;
    The roofs, that heard our earliest cry,
Will shelter one of stranger race.

We go, but ere we go from home,
    As down the garden-walks I move,
    Two spirits of a diverse love
Contend for loving masterdom.

One whispers, "Here thy boyhood sung
    Long since its matin song, and heard
    The low love-language of the bird
In native hazels tassel-hung."

The other answers, "Yea, but here
    Thy feet have stray'd in after hours
    With thy lost friend among the bowers,
And this hath made them trebly dear."

These two have striven half the day,
    And each prefers his separate claim,
    Poor rivals in a losing game,
That will not yield each other way.

I turn to go: my feet are set
    To leave the pleasant fields and farms;
    They mix in one another's arms
To one pure image of regret.

ELIZABETH GASKELL
1810–1865

Elizabeth Gaskell (née Stevenson) was an English novelist and biographer. Today she is recognized for her careful critique of difficult social problems, including class and contemporary attitudes to women. Her novel *North and South* (1854) illuminates the different ways of life and assorted social problems that occupy the traditional rural south and the modern suburban north. The majority of the novel is set in the fictional industrial town of Milton, which her protagonist Margaret Hale moves to after leaving the village of Helstone near the south coast. The two places are set in sharp contrast to one another. This extract from the beginning of the novel shows how Margaret feels completely free when she is out of doors.

from *North and South*

It was the latter part of July when Margaret returned home. The forest trees were all one dark, full, dusky green; the fern below them caught all the slanting sunbeams; the weather was sultry and broodingly still. Margaret used to tramp along by her father's side, crushing down the fern with a cruel glee, as she felt it yield under her light foot, and send up the fragrance peculiar to it—out on the broad commons into the warm scented light, seeing multitudes of wild, free, living creatures, revelling in the sunshine, and the herbs and flowers it called forth. This life—at least these walks—realised all Margaret's anticipations. She took a pride in her forest. Its people were her people. She made hearty friends with them; learned and delighted in using their peculiar words; took up her freedom amongst them; nursed their babies; talked or read with slow distinctness to their old people; carried dainty messes to their sick; resolved before long to teach at the school, where her father went every day as to an appointed task, but she was continually tempted off to go and see some individual friend—man, woman, or child—in some cottage in the green shade of the forest. Her out-of-doors life was perfect. Her indoors life had its drawbacks. With the healthy shame of a child, she blamed herself for her keenness of sight, in perceiving that all was not as it should be there. Her mother—her mother always so kind and tender towards her—seemed now and then so much discontented with their situation; thought that the bishop strangely neglected his episcopal duties, in not giving Mr. Hale a better living; and almost reproached her husband because he could not bring himself to say that he wished to leave the parish, and undertake the charge of a larger. He would sigh aloud as he answered, that if he could do what he ought in little Helstone, he should be thankful; but every day he was more overpowered; the world became more bewildering. At each repeated urgency of his wife, that he would put himself in the way of seeking some preferment, Margaret saw that her father shrank more and more; and she strove at such times to reconcile her mother to Helstone. Mrs. Hale said that the near neighbourhood of so many trees affected her health; and Margaret would try to tempt her forth on to the beautiful, broad, upland, sun-streaked, cloud-shadowed common; for she was sure that her mother had accustomed herself too much to an in-doors life, seldom extending her walks beyond the church, the school, and the neighbouring cottages. This did good for a time; but when the autumn drew on, and the weather became more changeable, her mother's idea of the unhealthiness of the place increased; and she repined even more frequently that her husband, who was more learned than Mr. Hume, a better parish priest than Mr. Houldsworth, should not have met with the preferment that these two former neighbours of theirs had done.

This marring of the peace of home, by long hours of discontent, was what Margaret was unprepared for. She knew, and had rather revelled in the idea, that she should have to give up many luxuries, which had only been troubles and trammels to her freedom in Harley Street. Her keen enjoyment of every sensuous pleasure, was balanced finely, if not over-balanced, by her conscious pride in being able to do without them all, if need were. But the cloud never comes in that quarter of the horizon from which we watch for it. There had been slight complaints and passing regrets on her mother's part, over some trifle connected with Helstone, and her father's position there, when Margaret had been spending her holidays at home before; but in the general happiness of the recollection of those times, she had forgotten the small details which were not so pleasant.

In the latter half of September, the autumnal rains and storms came on, and Margaret was obliged to remain more in the house than she had hitherto done. Helstone was at some distance from any neighbours of their own standard of cultivation.

"It is undoubtedly one of the most out-of-the-way places in England," said Mrs. Hale, in one of her plaintive moods. "I can't help regretting constantly that papa has really no one to associate with here; he is so thrown away; seeing no one but farmers and labourers from week's end to week's end. If we only lived at the other side of the parish, it would be something; there we should be almost within walking distance of the Stansfields; certainly the Gormans would be within a walk."

"Gormans," said Margaret. "Are those the Gormans who made their fortunes in trade at Southampton? Oh! I'm glad we don't visit them. I don't like shoppy people. I think we are far better off, knowing only cottagers and labourers, and people without pretence."

"You must not be so fastidious, Margaret, dear!" said her mother, secretly thinking of a young and handsome Mr. Gorman whom she had once met at Mr. Hume's.

"No! I call mine a very comprehensive taste; I like all people whose occupations have to do with land; I like soldiers and sailors, and the three learned professions, as they call them. I'm sure you don't want me to admire butchers and bakers, and candlestick-makers, do you, mamma?"

"But the Gormans were neither butchers nor bakers, but very respectable coach-builders."

"Very well. Coach-building is a trade all the same, and I think a much more useless one than that of butchers or bakers. Oh! how tired I used to be of the drives every day in Aunt Shaw's carriage, and how I longed to walk!"

And walk Margaret did, in spite of the weather. She was so happy out of doors, at her father's side, that she almost danced; and with the soft violence of the west wind behind her, as she crossed some heath, she seemed to be borne onwards, as lightly and easily as the fallen leaf that was wafted along by the autumnal breeze. But the evenings were rather difficult to fill up agreeably. Immediately after tea her father withdrew into his small library, and she and her mother were left alone. Mrs. Hale had never cared much for books, and had discouraged her husband, very early in their married life, in his desire of reading aloud to her, while she worked. At one time they had tried backgammon as a resource; but as Mr. Hale grew to take an increasing interest in his school and his parishioners, he found that the interruptions which arose out of these duties were regarded as hardships by his wife, not to be accepted as the natural conditions of his profession, but to be regretted and struggled against by her as they severally arose. So he withdrew, while the children were yet young, into his library, to spend his evenings (if he were at home), in reading the speculative and metaphysical books which were his delight.

MARK TWAIN
1835–1910

Samuel Langhorne Clemens, more commonly known by his pen name, Mark Twain, was an American writer and humorist. Widely known in his day for his wit and best remembered today for *The Adventures of Tom Sawyer* (1876) and *The Adventures of Huckleberry Finn* (1885), he was also the writer of a number of travel narratives, including *A Tramp Abroad* (1880). The satirical travelogue combines autobiography and fiction, and details a journey through Germany, Switzerland, France and Italy, based on a tour Clemens himself made in 1878. The driving force of satire in the book comes from the narrator's facetious persona, which Twain uses to poke fun at the stereotype of the American tourist. In this next extract, the narrator tells us that the joy of walking is in the talking – no matter how frivolous the topics may be, or how poorly informed the speakers.

from *A Tramp Abroad*

CHAPTER XXIII

We were satisfied that we could walk to Oppenau in one day, now that we were in practice, so we set out next morning after breakfast determined to do it. It was all the way down hill, and we had the loveliest summer weather for it. So we set the pedometer, and then stretched away on an easy, regular stride, down through the cloven forest, drawing in the fragrant breath of the morning in deep refreshing draughts, and wishing we might never have anything to do for ever but walk to Oppenau, and keep on doing it, and then doing it over again.

Now the true charm of pedestrianism does not lie in the walking, or in the scenery, but in the talking. The walking is good to time the movement of the tongue by, and to keep the blood and the brain stirred up and active; the scenery and the woodsy smells are good to bear in upon a man an unconscious and unobtrusive charm and solace to eye and soul and sense; but the supreme pleasure comes from the talk. It is no matter whether one talks wisdom or nonsense, the case is the same; the bulk of the enjoyment lies in the wagging of the gladsome jaw and the flapping of the sympathetic ear.

And what a motley variety of subjects a couple of

people will casually rake over in the course of a day's tramp! There being no constraint, a change of subject is always in order, and so a body is not likely to keep pegging at a single topic until it grows tiresome. We discussed everything we knew, during the first fifteen or twenty minutes, that morning, and then branched out into the glad, free, boundless realm of the things we were not certain about.

CHRISTOPHER MORLEY
1890–1957

Born in Pennsylvania in the US, Christopher Morley was a journalist, essayist, poet and theatre producer. His essay collection *Travels in Philadelphia* (1920) frequently asserts that whether in city or country, the best way to see the world is on foot. The following extract from his essay 'Sauntering' complements ideas that he expounds elsewhere in his oeuvre, for example in his essay 'On Laziness', where he argues against busyness and for a slower pace of life. In 'Sauntering' he argues that there is a great deal of satisfaction and sheer 'life' in being a 'saunterer', that is, the idle pedestrian who takes great satisfaction in observing the world, who follows the impulse of what he calls the 'everlasting lure of round-the-corner', where the aim is simply 'to catch a passing snapshot' of existence and to savour it. He argues that we don't need to make a Henry Thoreau-style retreat to enjoy this.

from 'Sauntering'

Some famous lady—who was it?—used to say of anyone she richly despised that he was "a saunterer." I suppose she meant he was a mere trifler, a lounger, an idle stroller of the streets. It is an ignominious confession, but I am a confirmed saunterer. I love to be set down haphazard among unknown byways; to saunter with open eyes, watching the moods and humors of men, the shapes of their dwellings, the criss-cross of their streets. It is an implanted passion that grows keener and keener. The everlasting lure of round-the-corner, how fascinating it is!

I love city squares. The most interesting persons are always those who have nothing special to do: children, nurses, policemen, and actors at 11 o'clock in the morning. These are always to be found in the park; by which I mean not an enormous sector of denatured countryside with bridle paths, fishponds and sea lions, but some broad patch of turf in a shabby elbow of the city, striped with pavements, with plenty of sun-warmed benches and a cast-iron zouave erected about 1873 to remind one of the horrors of commemorative statuary. Children scuffle to and fro; dusty men with spiculous chins loll on the seats; the uncouth and pathetic vibrations of humankind are on every side.

It is entrancing to walk in such places and catalogue all that may be seen. I jot down on scraps of paper a list of all the shops on a side street; the names of tradesmen that amuse me; the absurd repartees of gutter children. Why? It amuses me and that is sufficient excuse. From now until the end of time no one else will ever see life with my eyes, and I mean to make the most of my chance. Just as Thoreau compiled a Domesday Book and kind of classified directory of the sights, sounds and scents of Walden (carefully recording the manners of a sandbank and the prejudices of a woodlouse or an apple tree) so I love to annotate the phenomena of the city. I can be as solitary in a city street as ever Thoreau was in Walden.

And no Walden sky was ever more blue than the roof of Washington square this morning. Sitting here reading Thoreau I am entranced by the mellow flavor of the young summer. The sun is just goodly enough to set the being in a gentle toasting muse. The trees confer together in a sleepy whisper. I have had buckwheat cakes and syrup for breakfast, and eggs fried both recto and verso; good foundation for speculation. I puff cigarettes and am at peace with myself. Many a worthy waif comes to lounge beside me; he glances at my scuffed boots, my baggy trousers; he knows me for one of the fraternity. By their boots ye shall know them. Many of those who have abandoned the race for this world's honors have a shrewdness all their own. What is it Thoreau says, with his penetrative truth?—"Sometimes we are inclined to class those who are once and a half witted with the half witted, because we appreciate only a third part of their wit." By the time a man is thirty he should be able to see what life has to offer, and take what dishes on the menu agree with him best. That is whole wit, indeed, or wit-and-a-half. And if he finds his pleasure on a park bench in ragged trousers let him lounge then, with good heart. I welcome him to the goodly fellowship of saunterers, an acolyte of the excellent church of the agorolaters!

FREDERICK DOUGLASS
1818–1895

Frederick Douglass was an African American writer, orator, social reformer, intellectual, statesman and leader of the abolitionist movement. His autobiography *Narrative of the Life of Frederick Douglass, an American Slave* (1845) records his experiences of being born into slavery in Maryland, USA. At a time when white American authors were waxing lyrical about the freedom and joy of walking for leisure, this next extract from Frederick's account reminds us that individuals in the same nation were denied these privileges. He describes an eight-mile walk that he undertakes in order to seek protection reminding us how walking was not always such a joy but a tool of survival.

from *Narrative of the Life of*
Frederick Douglass

I have already intimated that my condition was much worse during the first six months of my stay at Mr. Covey's, than in the last six. The circumstances leading to the change in Mr. Covey's course toward me form an epoch in my humble history. You have seen how man was made a slave; you shall see how a slave was made a man. On one of the hottest days of the month of August, 1833, Bill Smith, William Hughes, a slave named Eli, and myself, were engaged in fanning wheat. Hughes was clearing the fanned wheat from before the fan, Eli was turning, Smith was feeding, and I was carrying wheat to the fan. The work was simple, requiring strength rather than intellect; yet, to one entirely unused to such work, it came very hard. About three o'clock of that day, I broke down; my strength failed me; I was seized with a violent aching of the head, attended with extreme dizziness; I trembled in every limb. Finding what was coming, I nerved myself up, feeling it would never do to stop work. I stood as long as I could stagger to the hopper with grain. When I could stand no longer, I fell, and felt as if held down by some immense weight. The fan of course stopped; every one had his own work to do; and no one could do the work of the other, and have his own go on at the same time.

Mr. Covey was at the house, about one hundred yards from the treading-yard where we were fanning. On hearing the fan stop, he left immediately, and came to the spot where we were. He hastily enquired what the matter was. Bill answered that I was sick, and there was no one to bring wheat to the fan. I had by this time crawled away under the side of the post and rail-fence by which the yard was enclosed, hoping to find relief by getting out of the sun. He then asked where I was. He was told by one of the hands. He came to the spot, and after looking at me awhile, asked me what was the matter. I told him as well as I could, for I scarce had strength to speak. He then gave me a savage kick in the side, and told me to get up. I tried to do so, but fell back in the attempt. He gave me another kick, and again told me to rise. I again tried, and succeeded in gaining my feet: but, stooping to get the tub with which I was feeding the fan, I again staggered and fell. While down in this situation, Mr. Covey took up the hickory slat with which Hughes had been striking off the half-bushel measure, and with it gave me a heavy blow upon the head, making a large wound, and the blood ran freely; and with this, again told me to get up. I made no effort to comply, having now made up my mind to let him do his worst. In a short time after receiving this blow, my head grew better. Mr. Covey had now left me to my fate. At this moment I resolved, for the first time, to go to my master, enter a complaint, and ask his protection. In order to do this, I must that afternoon walk seven miles; and this, under the circumstances, was truly a severe undertaking. I was exceedingly feeble; made so as much by the kicks and blows which I received, as by the severe fit of sickness to which I had been subjected. I, however, watched my chance, while Covey was looking in an opposite direction, and started for St. Michael's. I succeeded in getting a considerable distance on my way to the woods, when Covey discovered me, and called after me to come back, threatening what he would do if I did not come. I disregarded both his calls and his threats, and made my way to the woods as fast as my feeble state would allow; and thinking I might be over-hauled by him if I kept the road, I walked through the woods, keeping far enough from the road to avoid detection, and near enough to prevent losing my way. I had not gone far, before my little strength again failed me. I could go no farther. I fell down, and lay for a considerable time. The blood was yet oozing from the wound on my head. For a time I thought I should bleed to death, and think now that

I should have done so, but that the blood so matted my hair as to stop the wound. After lying there about three quarters of an hour, I nerved myself up again, and started on my way, through bogs and briers, barefooted and bareheaded, tearing my feet sometimes at nearly every step; and after a journey of about seven miles, occupying some five hours to perform it, I arrived at master's store. I then presented an appearance enough to affect any but a heart of iron. From the crown of my head to my feet, I was covered with blood. My hair was all clotted with dust and blood; my shirt was stiff with blood. My legs and feet were torn in sundry places with briers and thorns, and were also covered with blood. I suppose I looked like a man who had escaped a den of wild beasts, and barely escaped them. In this state I appeared before my master, humbly entreating him to interpose his authority for my protection. I told him all the circumstances as well as I could, and it seemed, as I spoke, at times to affect him. He would then walk the floor, and seek to justify Covey by saying he expected I deserved it. He asked me what I wanted. I told him to let me get a new home; that as sure as I lived with Mr. Covey again, I should live with but to die with him; that Covey would surely kill me—he was in a fair way for it. Master Thomas ridiculed the idea that there was any danger of Mr. Covey's killing me, and said that he knew Mr. Covey; that he was a good man, and that he could not think of taking me from him; that should he do so, he would lose the whole year's wages; that I belonged to Mr. Covey for one year, and that I must go back to him, come what might; and that I must not trouble him with any more stories, or that he would himself *get hold of me*. After threatening me thus, he gave me a very large dose of salts, telling me that I might remain in St. Michael's that night, (it being quite late,) but that I must be off back to Mr. Covey's early in the morning; and that if I did not, he would *get hold of me*, which meant that he would whip me. I remained all night, and according to his orders, I started off to Covey's in the morning, (Saturday morning), wearied in body and broken in spirit. I got no supper that night, or breakfast that morning. I reached Covey's about nine o'clock; and just as I was getting over the fence that divided Mrs. Kemp's fields from ours, out ran Covey with his cowskin, to give me another whipping. Before he could reach me, I succeeded in getting to the corn-field; and as the corn was very high, it afforded me the means of hiding. He seemed very angry, and searched for me a long time. My behaviour was altogether unaccountable. He finally gave up the chase, thinking, I suppose, that I must come home for something to eat; he would give himself no further trouble in looking for me. I spent that day mostly in the woods, having the alternative before me—to go home and be whipped to death, or stay in the woods and be starved to death. That night, I fell in with Sandy Jenkins, a slave with whom I was somewhat acquainted. Sandy had a free wife, who lived about four miles from Mr. Covey's; and it being Saturday, he was on his way to see her. I told him my circumstances, and he very kindly invited me to go home with him. I went home with him, and talked this whole matter over, and got his advice as to what course it was best for me to pursue. I found Sandy an old adviser. He told me, with great solemnity, I must go back to Covey; but that before I went, I must go with him into another part of the woods, where there was a certain *root*, which, if I would take some of it with me, carrying it *always on my right side*, would render it impossible for Mr. Covey, or any other white man, to whip me. He said he had carried it for years; and since he had done so, he had never received a blow, and never expected to, while he carried it. I at first rejected the idea, that the simple carrying of a root in my pocket would have any such effect as he had said, and was not disposed to take it; but Sandy impressed the necessity with much earnestness, telling me it could do no harm, i it did no good. To please him, I at length took the root, and, according to his direction, carried it upon my right side. This was Sunday morning. I immediately started for home; and upon entering the yard gate, out came Mr. Covey on his way to meeting. He spoke to me very kindly, bade me drive the pigs from a lot near by, and passed on towards the church. Now this singular conduct of Mr. Covey really made me begin to think that there was something in the *root* which Sandy had given me; and had it been on any other day than Sunday, I could have attributed the conduct to no other cause than the influence of that root; and as it was, I was half inclined to think the *root* to be something more than I at first had taken it to be. All went well till Monday morning.

LESLIE STEPHEN
1832–1904

Leslie Stephen is perhaps best known today for being the father of author Virginia Woolf and designer Vanessa Bell. He was, however, an English writer, critic, historian and a prominent biographer in his own right. He was also a keen mountaineer and president of the first-ever mountaineering club – the Alpine Club – for several years. His enthusiasm for walking is evident in the following extract from his essay 'In Praise of Walking' (1898). Walking, according to Stephen, facilitates a meeting of the mind and the body, accessible to everyone, both high and low. Additionally, he raises the interesting idea that individual walks can serve a useful role as chapter markers in our memories, which encapsulate the emotional and mental state of the walker at a particular point in time, a kind of pit stop on an individual's broader journey, the 'earthly pilgrimage'.

from 'In Praise of Walking'

As a man grows old, he is told by some moralists that he may find consolation for increasing infirmities in looking back upon a well-spent life. No doubt such a retrospect must be very agreeable, but the question must occur to many of us whether our life offers the necessary materials for self-complacency. What part of it, if any, has been well spent? To that I find it convenient to reply, for my own purposes, any part in which I thoroughly enjoyed myself. If it be proposed to add 'innocently,' I will not quarrel with the amendment. Perhaps, indeed, I may have a momentary regret for some pleasures which do not quite deserve that epithet, but the pleasure of which I am about to speak is obtrusively and pre-eminently innocent. Walking is among recreations what ploughing and fishing are among industrial labours: it is primitive and simple; it brings us into contact with mother earth and unsophisticated nature; it requires no elaborate apparatus and no extraneous excitement. It is fit even for poets and philosophers, and he who can thoroughly enjoy it must have at least some capacity for worshipping the 'cherub Contemplation.' He must be able to enjoy his own society without the factitious stimulants of the more violent physical recreations. I have always been a humble admirer of athletic excellence. I retain, in spite of much head-shaking from wise educationalists, my early vener-ation for the heroes of the river and the cricket-field. To me they have still the halo which surrounded them in the days when 'muscular Christianity' was first preached and the whole duty of man said to consist in fearing God and walking a thousand miles in a thou-sand hours. I rejoice unselfishly in these later days to see the stream of bicyclists restoring animation to deserted highroads or to watch even respected con-temporaries renewing their youth in the absorbing delights of golf. While honouring all genuine delight in manly exercises, I regret only the occasional admixture of lower motives which may lead to its degeneration. Now it is one merit of walking that its real devotees are little exposed to such temptations. Of course there are such things as professional pedes-trians making 'records' and seeking the applause of the mob. When I read of the immortal Captain Barclay performing his marvellous feats, I admire respectfully, but I fear that his motives included a greater admixture of vanity than of the emotions con-genial to the higher intellect. The true walker is one to whom the pursuit is in itself delightful; who is not indeed priggish enough to be above a certain compla-cency in the physical prowess required for his pursuit but to whom the muscular effort of the legs is subsidi ary to the 'cerebration' stimulated by the effort; to the quiet musings and imaginings which arise most spontaneously as he walks, and generate the intellectual harmony which is the natural accompaniment to the monotonous tramp of his feet. The cyclist or the golf-player, I am told, can hold such intercourse with himself in the intervals of striking the ball or working his machine. But the true pedestrian loves walking because, so far from distracting his mind, it is favourable to the equable and abundant flow of tranquil and half-conscious meditation. Therefore I should be sorry if the pleasures of cycling or any other recreation tended to put out of fashion the habit of the good old walking-tour.

For my part, when I try to summon up remembrance of 'well-spent' moments, I find myself taking a kind of inverted view of the past; inverted, that is, so far as the accidental becomes the essential. If I turn over the intellectual album which memory is always compiling, I find that the most distinct pictures which it contains are those of old walks. Other memories of incomparably greater intrinsic value coalesce into wholes. They are more massive but less distinct. The memory of a friendship that has brightened one's whole life survives not as a series of incidents but as a general impression of the friend's characteristic qualities due to the superposition of innumerable forgotten pictures. I remember him, not the specific conversations by which he revealed himself. The memories of walks, on the other hand, are all localised and dated; they are hitched on to particular times and places; they spontaneously form a kind of calendar or connecting thread upon which other memories may be strung. As I look back, a long series of little vignettes presents itself, each representing a definite stage of my earthly pilgrimage summed up and embodied in a walk. Their background of scenery recalls places once familiar, and the thoughts associated with the places revive thoughts of the contemporary occupations. The labour of scribbling books happily leaves no distinct impression, and I would forget that it had ever been undergone; but the picture of some delightful ramble includes incidentally a reference to the nightmare of literary toil from which it relived me. The author is but the accidental appendage of the tramp. My days are bound each to each not by 'natural piety' (or not, let me say, by natural piety alone) but by pedestrian enthusiasm. The memory of school days, if one may trust to the usual reminiscences, generally clusters round a flogging, or some solemn words from the spiritual teacher instilling the seed of a guiding principle of life. I remember a sermon or two rather ruefully; and I confess to memories of a flogging so unjust that am even now stung by the thought of it. But what comes most spontaneously to my mind is the memory of certain strolls, 'out of bounds,' when I could forget the Latin grammar, and enjoy such a sense of the beauties of nature as is embodied for a child in a pond haunted by water-rats, or a field made romantic by threats of 'man-traps and spring-guns.' Then, after a crude fashion, one was becoming more or less of a reflecting and individual being, not a mere automaton set in movement by pedagogic machinery.

The day on which I was fully initiated into the mysteries is marked by a white stone. It was when I put on a knapsack and started from Heidelberg for a march through the Odenwald. Then I first knew the delightful sensation of independence and detachment enjoyed during a walking tour. Free from all bothers of railway time-tables and extraneous machinery, you trust to your own legs, stop when you please, diverge into any track that takes your fancy, and drop in upon some quaint variety of human life at every inn where you put up for the night. You share for the time the mood in which Borrow settled down in the dingle after escaping from his bondage in the publishers' London slums. You have no dignity to support, and the dress-coat of conventional life has dropped into oblivion, like the bundle from Christian's shoulders.

HARRIET MARTINEAU
1802–1876

Harriet Martineau was an English novelist, essayist, journalist, economic writer and social theorist who first rose to fame with her *Illustrations of Political Economy* (1832), a collection of short stories that illustrated economic science. She was a proto-feminist thinker who travelled widely, recording her experiences in books such as *Retrospect of Western Travel* (1838). The following two extracts give us two different perspectives on walking. In the extract from her novel *Deerbrook* (1838), walking in the countryside is an escape from the gossip of the village, where the protagonist, Margaret, and her sister are reduced to the sum of their romantic prospects. In this extract, the clever and quick-witted Margaret is challenged to walk out on the ice-covered river, where she falls in. Her comical, no-nonsense recovery from the incident paints her as a hardy female character, thick-skinned and capable in the face of physical difficulty. The second extract is taken from Martineau's *Autobiography* (1877), giving us an insight into how exercise can temporarily alleviate suffering and make life feel worth living.

144

from *Deerbrook*

For some little time Margaret had been practising the device, so familiar to the unhappy, of carrying off mental agitation by bodily exertion. She was now eager to be doing something more active than walking by Mrs. Grey's side, listening to ideas which she knew just as well without their being spoken. Mrs. Grey's thoughts about Mrs. Rowland, and Mrs. Rowland's ideas of Mrs. Grey, might always be anticipated by those who knew the ladies. Hester and Margaret had learned to think of something else, while this sort of comment was proceeding, and to resume their attention when it came to an end. Margaret had withdrawn from it now, and was upon the ice with Sydney.

"Why, cousin Margaret, you don't mean that you are afraid of walking on the ice?" cried Sydney, balancing himself on his heels. "Mr. Hope, what do you think of that?" he called out, as Hope skimmed past them. "Cousin Margaret is afraid of going on the ice!"

"What does she think can happen to her?" asked Mr. Hope, his last words vanishing in the distance.

"It looks so gray, and clear, and dark, Sydney."

"Pooh! It is thick enough between you and the

water. You would have to get down a good way, I can tell you, before you could get drowned."

"But it is so slippery!"

"What of that? What else did you expect with ice? If you tumble, you can get up again. I have been down three times this morning."

"Well, that is a great consolation, certainly. Which way do you want me to walk?"

"Oh, any way. Across the river to the other bank, if you like. You will remember next summer, when we come this way in a boat, that you have walked across the very place."

"That is true," said Margaret. "I will go if Sophia will go with me."

"There is no use in asking any of them," said Sydney. "They stand dawdling and looking, till their lips and noses are all blue and red, and they are never up to any fun."

"I will try as far as that pole first," said Margaret. "I should not care if they had not swept away all the snow here, so as to make the ice look so gray and slippery."

"That pole!" said Sydney. "Why, that pole is put up on purpose to show that you must not go there. Don't you see how the ice is broken all round it? Oh, I know how it is that you are so stupid and cowardly to-day. You've lived in Birmingham all your winters, and you've never been used to walk on the ice."

"I am glad you have found that out at last. Now, look—I am really going. What a horrid sensation!" she cried, as she cautiously put down one foot before the other on the transparent floor. She did better when she reached the middle of the river, where the ice had been ground by the skates.

"Now, you would get on beautifully," said Sydney, "if you would not look at your feet. Why can't you look at the people, and the trees opposite?"

"Suppose I should step into a hole."

"There are no holes. Trust me for the holes. What do you flinch so for? The ice always cracks so, in one part or another. I thought you had been shot."

"So did I," said she, laughing. "But, Sydney, we are a long way from both banks."

"To be sure: that is what we came for."

Margaret looked somewhat timidly about her. An indistinct idea flitted through her mind—how glad she should be to be accidentally, innocently drowned; and scarcely recognising it, she proceeded.

"You get on well," shouted Mr. Hope, as he flew past, on his return up the river.

"There, now," said Sydney, presently; "it is a very little way to the bank. I will just take a trip up and down, and come for you again, to go back; and then we will try whether we can't get cousin Hester over, when she sees you have been safe there and back."

This was a sight which Hester was not destined to behold. Margaret had an ignorant partiality for the ice which was the least gray; and, when left to herself, she made for a part which looked less like glass. Nobody particularly heeded her. She slipped, and recovered herself: she slipped again, and fell, hearing the ice crack under her. Every time she attempted to rise, she found the place too slippery to keep her feet; next, there was a hole under her; she felt the cold water—she was sinking through; she caught at the surrounding edges—they broke away. There was a cry from the bank, just as the death-cold waters seemed to close all round her, and she felt the ice like a heavy weight above her. One thought of joy—"It will soon be all over now"—was the only experience she was conscious of.

In two minutes more, she was breathing the air again, sitting on the bank, and helping to wring out her clothes. How much may pass in two minutes! Mr. Hope was coming up the river again, when he saw a bustle on the bank, and slipped off his skates, to be ready to be of service. He ran as others ran, and arrived just when a dark-blue dress was emerging from the water, and then a dripping fur tippet, and then the bonnet, making the gradual revelation to him who it was. For one instant he covered his face with his hands, half-hiding an expression of agony so intense that a bystander who saw it, said, "Take comfort, sir: she has been in but a very short time. She'll recover, I don't doubt." Hope leaped to the bank, and received her from the arms of the men who had drawn her out. The first thing she remembered was hearing, in the lowest tone she could conceive of—"Oh, God! my Margaret!" and a groan, which she felt rather than heard. Then there were many warm and busy hands about her head—removing her bonnet, shaking out her hair, and chafing her temples. She sighed out, "Oh, dear!" and she heard that soft groan again. In another moment she roused herself, sat up, saw Hope's convulsed countenance, and Sydney standing motionless and deadly pale.

"I shall never forgive myself," she heard her brother exclaim.

"Oh, I am very well," said she, remembering all about it. "The air feels quite warm. Give me my bonnet. I can walk home."

from *Autobiography*

My health gave way, more and more; and my suffering throughout the year 1827 from the pain which came on every evening was such as it is disagreeable to think of now. For pain of body and mind it was truly a terrible year, though it had its satisfactions, one of the chief of which was a long visit which I paid to my brother Robert and his wife (always a dear friend of mine to this day) at their home in Dudley. I remember our walks in the grounds of Dudley Castle, and the organ-playing at home, after my brother's business hours, and the inexhaustible charm of the baby, as gleams amidst the darkness of that season. I found then the unequalled benefit of long solitary walks in such a case as mine. I had found it even at Norwich, in midwinter, when all was bleak on that exposed level country; and now, amidst the beauty which surrounds Dudley, there was no end of my walks or of my relish for them; and I always came home with a cheered and lightened heart. Such poetry as I wrote (I can't bear to think of it) I wrote in those days.

THOMAS HARDY
1840–1928

Thomas Hardy was an English novelist and poet whose work was primarily focused on the lives and struggles of individuals in the rural communities in the south-west of England, his native region, which he fictionalized as Wessex. In his poem 'At Castle Boterel', we see how walking can open up fertile ground for emotional intimacy and openness. As the narrator walks through the hills in the present, he is simultaneously transported back to a time when he walked the same route with a former lover. In the second extract, taken from *Far from the Madding Crowd* (1874), the independent protagonist Bathsheba Everdene performs her nightly patrol of the boundaries of her land. In the darkness of the woods, hidden from the rest of the world, she meets the dashing Sergeant Troy.

'At Castle Boterel'

As I drive to the junction of lane and highway,
    And the drizzle bedrenches the waggonette,
I look behind at the fading byway,
    And see on its slope, now glistening wet,
        Distinctly yet

Myself and a girlish form benighted
    In dry March weather. We climb the road
Beside a chaise. We had just alighted
    To ease the sturdy pony's load
        When he sighed and slowed.

What we did as we climbed, and what we talked of
    Matters not much, nor to what it led—
Something that life will not be balked of
    Without rude reason till hope is dead,
        And feeling fled.

It filled but a minute. But was there ever
    A time of such quality, since or before,
In that hill's story? To one mind never,
    Though it has been climbed, foot-swift, foot-sore,
        By thousands more.

Primaeval rocks form the road's steep border,
    And much have they faced there, first and last,
Of the transitory in Earth's long order;
    But what they record in colour and cast
        Is—that we two passed.

And to me, though Time's unflinching rigour,
    In mindless rote, has ruled from sight
The substance now, one phantom figure
    Remains on the slope, as when that night
        Saw us alight.

I look and see it there, shrinking, shrinking,
    I look back at it amid the rain
For the very last time; for my sand is sinking,
    And I shall traverse old love's domain
        Never again.

from *Far from the Madding Crowd*

CHAPTER XXIV

THE SAME NIGHT—THE FIR PLANTATION

Among the multifarious duties which Bathsheba had voluntarily imposed upon herself by dispensing with the services of a bailiff, was the particular one of looking round the homestead before going to bed, to see that all was right and safe for the night. Gabriel had almost constantly preceded her in this tour every evening, watching her affairs as carefully as any specially appointed officer of surveillance could have done; but this tender devotion was to a great extent unknown to his mistress, and as much as was known was somewhat thanklessly received. Women are never tired of bewailing man's fickleness in love, but they only seem to snub his constancy.

As watching is best done invisibly, she usually carried a dark lantern in her hand, and every now and then turned on the light to examine nooks and corners with the coolness of a metropolitan police-man. This coolness may have owed its existence not so much to her fearlessness of expected danger as to her freedom from the suspicion of any; her worst anticipated discovery being that a horse might not be well bedded, the fowls not all in, or a door not closed.

This night the buildings were inspected as usual, and she went round to the farm paddock. Here the only sounds disturbing the stillness were steady munchings of many mouths, and stentorian breathings from all but invisible noses, ending in snores and puffs like the blowing of bellows slowly. Then the munching would recommence, when the lively imagination might assist the eye to discern a group of pink-white nostrils shaped as caverns, and very clammy and humid on their surfaces, not exactly pleasant to the touch until one got used to them; the mouths beneath having a great partiality for closing upon any loose end of Bathsheba's apparel which came within reach of their tongues. Above each of these a still keener vision suggested a brown forehead and two staring thought not unfriendly eyes, and above all a pair of whitish crescent-shaped horns like two particularly new moons, an occasional stolid 'moo!' proclaiming beyond the shade of a doubt that these phenomena were the features and persons of Daisy, Whitefoot, Bonny-lass, Jolly-O, Spot, Twinkle-eye, etc., etc.—the respectable dairy of Devon cows belonging to Bathsheba aforesaid.

Her way back to the house was by a path through a young plantation of tapering firs, which had been planted some years earlier to shelter the premises from the north wind. By reason of the density of the interwoven foliage overhead it was gloomy there at cloudless noontide, twilight in the evening, dark as midnight at dusk, and black as the ninth plague of Egypt at midnight. To describe the spot is to call it a vast, low, naturally formed hall, the plumy ceiling of which was supported by slender pillars of living wood, the floor being covered with a soft dun carpet of dead spikelets and mildewed cones, with a tuft of grass-blades here and there.

This bit of the path was always the crux of the night's ramble, though, before starting, her apprehensions of danger were not vivid enough to lead her to take a companion. Slipping along here covertly as Time, Bathsheba fancied she could hear footsteps entering the track at the opposite end. It was certainly a rustle of footsteps. Her own instantly fell as gently as snowflakes. She reassured herself by a remembrance that the path was public, and that the traveller was probably some villager returning home; regretting, at the same time, that the meeting should be about to occur in the darkest point of her route, even though only just outside her own door.

The noise approached, came close, and a figure was apparently on the point of gliding past her when something tugged at her skirt and pinned it forcibly to the ground. The instantaneous check nearly threw

Bathsheba off her balance. In recovering she struck against warm clothes and buttons.

'A rum start, upon my soul!' said a masculine voice, a foot or so above her head. 'Have I hurt you, mate?'

'No,' said Bathsheba, attempting to shrink away.

'We have got hitched together somehow, I think.'

'Yes.'

'Are you a woman?'

'Yes.'

'A lady, I should have said.'

'It doesn't matter.'

'I am a man.'

'Oh!'

Bathsheba softly tugged again, but to no purpose.

'Is that a dark lantern you have? I fancy so,' said the man.

'Yes.'

'If you'll allow me I'll open it, and set you free.'

A hand seized the lantern, the door was opened, the rays burst out from their prison, and Bathsheba beheld her position with astonishment.

The man to whom she was hooked was brilliant in brass and scarlet. He was a soldier. His sudden appearance was to darkness what the sound of a trumpet is to silence. Gloom, the *genius loci* at all times hitherto, was now totally overgrown, less by the lantern-light than by what the lantern lighted. The contrast of this revelation with her anticipations of some sinister figure in sombre garb was so great that it had upon her the effect of a fairy transformation.

It was immediately apparent that the military man's spur had become entangled in the gimp which decorated the skirt of her dress. He caught a view of her face.

'I'll unfasten you in one moment, miss,' he said, with newborn gallantry.

'O no—I can do it, thank you,' she hastily replied, and stooped for the performance.

The unfastening was not such a trifling affair. The rowel of the spur had so wound itself among the gimp cords in those few moments, that separation was likely to be a matter of time.

He too stooped, and the lantern standing on the ground betwixt them threw the gleam from its open side among the fir-tree needles and the blades of long damp grass with the effect of a large glowworm. It radiated upwards into their faces, and sent over half the plantation gigantic shadows of both man and woman, each dusky shape becoming distorted and mangled upon the tree-trunks till it wasted to nothing.

He looked hard into her eyes when she raised

them for a moment; Bathsheba looked down again, for his gaze was too strong to be received point-blank with her own. But she had obliquely noticed that he was young and slim, and that he wore three chevrons upon his sleeve.

Bathsheba pulled again.

'You are a prisoner, miss; it is no use blinking the matter,' said the soldier drily. 'I must cut your dress if you are in such a hurry.'

'Yes—please do!' she exclaimed helplessly.

'It wouldn't be necessary if you could wait a moment'; and he unwound a cord from the little wheel. She withdrew her own hand, but, whether by accident or design, he touched it. Bathsheba was vexed; she hardly knew why.

His unravelling went on, but it nevertheless seemed coming to no end. She looked at him again.

'Thank you for the sight of such a beautiful face!' said the young sergeant, without ceremony.

She coloured with embarrassment. ''Twas unwill-ingly shown,' she replied stiffly, and with as much dignity—which was very little—as she could infuse into a position of captivity.

'I like you the better for that incivility, miss,' he said.

'I should have liked—I wish—you had never shown yourself to me by intruding here!' She pulled

159

again, and the gathers of her dress began to give way like lilliputian musketry.

'I deserve the chastisement your words give me. But why should such a fair and dutiful girl have such an aversion to her father's sex?'

'Go on your way, please.'

'What, Beauty, and drag you after me? Do but look; I never saw such a tangle!'

'O, 'tis shameful of you; you have been making it worse on purpose to keep me here—you have!'

'Indeed, I don't think so,' said the sergeant, with a merry twinkle.

'I tell you you have!' she exclaimed, in high temper. 'I insist upon undoing it. Now, allow me!'

'Certainly, miss; I am not of steel.' He added a sigh which had as much archness in it as a sigh could possess without losing its nature altogether. 'I am thankful for beauty, even when 'tis thrown to me like a bone to a dog. These moments will be over too soon!'

She closed her lips in a determined silence.

Bathsheba was revolving in her mind whether by a bold and desperate rush she could free herself at the risk of leaving her skirt bodily behind her. The thought was too dreadful. The dress—which she had put on to appear stately at the supper—was the head and front of her wardrobe; not another in her stock became her so well. What woman in Bathsheba's position, not naturally timid, and within call of her retainers, would have bought escape from a dashing soldier at so dear a price?

❦

EMILY BRONTË
1818–1848

Emily Brontë was an English poet and author, best known for her only novel *Wuthering Heights* (1847). At the start of the novel, the young protagonist, Cathy, who has 'a taste for . . . solitary rambling', is restricted to walking in the grounds of her home, the Thrushcross Grange estate, but she longs to explore the moors. She is particularly intrigued by a set of rocky hills on the horizon known as Peniston Crags, beyond which she will eventually discover Wuthering Heights estate, home to her cousin Hareton and the enigmatic Heathcliff. In this extract, Cathy disobeys orders and leaves the estate, forcing the maid and narrator, Nelly, to set out on foot to retrieve her. The moors eventually become Cathy and Heathcliff's sanctuary from the two oppressive houses, despite the fact that the landscape is simultaneously presented as foreboding, supernatural and responsible for stirring up strange, wild sensations in Cathy.

from *Wuthering Heights*

Till she reached the age of thirteen, she had not once been beyond the range of the park by herself. Mr. Linton would take her with him a mile or so outside, on rare occasions; but he trusted her to no one else. Gimmerton was an unsubstantial name in her ears; the chapel, the only building she had approached or entered, except her own home. Wuthering Heights and Mr. Heathcliff did not exist for her: she was a perfect recluse; and, apparently, perfectly contented. Sometimes, indeed, while surveying the country from her nursery window, she would observe—

"Ellen, how long will it be before I can walk to the top of those hills? I wonder what lies on the other side—is it the sea?"

"No, Miss Cathy," I would answer; "it is hills again, just like these."

"And what are those golden rocks like when you stand under them?" she once asked.

The abrupt descent of Peniston Crags particularly attracted her notice; especially when the setting sun shone on it and the topmost heights, and the whole extent of landscape, besides, lay in shadow.

I explained that they were bare masses of stone,

with hardly enough earth in their clefts to nourish a stunted tree.

"And why are they bright so long after it is evening here?" she pursued.

"Because they are a great deal higher up than we are," replied I; "you could not climb them, they are so high and steep. In winter the frost is always there before it comes to us; and deep into summer I have found snow under that black hollow on the north-east side!"

"Oh, you have been on them!" she cried gleefully. "Then I can go, too, when I am a woman. Has papa been, Ellen?"

"Papa would tell you, miss," I answered hastily, "that they were not worth the trouble of visiting. The moors, where you ramble with him, are much nicer; and Thrushcross Park is the finest place in the world."

"But I know the park, and I don't know those," she murmured to herself. "And I should delight to look round me from the brow of that tallest point— my little pony Minny shall take me some time."

One of the maids mentioning the Fairy Cave, quite turned her head with a desire to fulfil this project. She teased Mr. Linton about it; and he promised she should have the journey when she got older. But Miss Catherine measured her age by months and—

"Now am I old enough to go to Peniston Crags?" was the constant question in her mouth.

The road thither wound close by Wuthering Heights. Edgar had not the heart to pass it; so she received as constantly the answer—

"Not yet, love; not yet."

I said Mrs. Heathcliff lived above a dozen years after quitting her husband. Her family were of a delicate constitution: she and Edgar both lacked the ruddy health that you will generally meet in these parts. What her last illness was, I am not certain; I conjecture they died of the same thing—a kind of fever, slow at its commencement, but incurable, and rapidly consuming life towards the close.

She wrote to inform her brother of the probable conclusion of a four months' indisposition under which she had suffered, and entreated him to come to her, if possible, for she had much to settle, and she wished to bid him adieu, and deliver Linton safely into his hands. Her hope was, that Linton might be left with him, as he had been with her; his father, she would fain convince herself, had no desire to assume the burden of his maintenance or education.

My master hesitated not a moment in complying with her request. Reluctant as he was to leave home at ordinary calls, he flew to answer this; commending Catherine to my peculiar vigilance, in his absence, with reiterated orders that she must not wander out of the park, even under my escort! He did not calculate on her going unaccompanied.

He was away three weeks. The first day or two, my charge sat in a corner of the library, too sad for either reading or playing: in that quiet state she caused me little trouble; but it was succeeded by an interval of impatient fretful weariness; and being too busy and too old then to run up and down amusing her, I hit on a method by which she might entertain herself.

I used to send her on her travels round the grounds—now on foot, and now on a pony; indulging her with a patient audience of all her real and imaginary adventures when she returned.

The summer shone in full prime: and she took such a taste for this solitary rambling that she often contrived to remain out from breakfast till tea; and then the evenings were spent in recounting her fanciful tales. I did not fear her breaking bounds; because the gates were generally locked, and I thought she would scarcely venture forth alone, if they had stood wide open.

Unluckily, my confidence proved misplaced. Catherine came to me one morning, at eight o'clock, and said she was that day an Arabian merchant going to cross the desert with his caravan; and I must give her plenty of provisions for herself and beasts: a horse and three camels, personated by a large hound and a couple of pointers.

I got together a good store of dainties, and slung them in a basket on one side of the saddle; and she sprang up as gay as a fairy, sheltered by her wide-brimmed hat and gauze veil from the July sun, and trotted off with a merry laugh, mocking my cautious counsel to avoid galloping, and come back early.

The naughty thing never made her appearance at tea. One traveller, the hound, being an old dog and fond of its ease, returned; but neither Cathy, nor the pony, nor the two pointers were visible in any direction, and I despatched emissaries down this path, and that path, and at last went wandering in search of her myself.

There was a labourer working at a fence round a plantation, on the borders of the grounds. I inquired of him if he had seen our young lady.

"I saw her at morn," he replied; "she would have me to cut her a hazel switch, and then she leapt her Galloway over the hedge yonder, where it is lowest, and galloped out of sight."

You may guess how I felt at hearing this news. It struck me directly she must have started for Penis-ton Crags. "What will become of her?" I ejaculated, pushing through a gap which the man was repairing, and making straight to the high road.

I walked as if for a wager, mile after mile, till a turn brought me in view of the Heights, but no Catherine could I detect far or near.

The Crags lie about a mile and a half beyond Mr. Heathcliff's place, and that is four from the Grange, so I began to fear night would fall ere I could reach them.

"And what if she should have slipped in clambering among them," I reflected, "and been killed, or broken some of her bones?" My suspense was truly painful; and, at first, it gave me delightful relief to observe, in hurrying by the farmhouse, Charlie, the fiercest of the pointers, lying under a window with swelled head and bleeding ear.

I unfastened the wicket and ran to the door, knocking vehemently for admittance. A woman whom I knew, and who formerly lived at Gimmerton, answered—she had been servant there since the death of Mr. Earnshaw.

"Ah," said she, "you are come a seeking your little mistress! don't be frightened, she's here safe: but I'm glad it isn't the master."

"He is not at home then, is he?" I panted, quite breathless with quick walking and alarm.

"No, no," she replied: "both he and Joseph are off, and I think they won't return this hour or more. Step in and rest you a bit."

I entered, and beheld my stray lamb seated on the hearth, rocking herself in a little chair that had been her mother's when a child. Her hat was hung against the wall, and she seemed perfectly at home, laughing and chattering, in the best spirits imaginable, to Hareton—now a great strong lad of eighteen—who stared at her with considerable curiosity and astonishment, comprehending precious little of the fluent succession of remarks and questions which her tongue never ceased pouring forth.

"Very well, miss!" I exclaimed, concealing my joy under an angry countenance. "This is your last ride till papa comes back. I'll not trust you over the threshold again, you naughty, naughty girl!"

"Aha, Ellen!" she cried gaily, jumping up and running to my side. "I shall have a pretty story to tell to-night; and so you've found me out. Have you ever been here in your life before?"

"Put that hat on, and home at once," said I. "I'm dreadfully grieved at you, Miss Cathy: you've done extremely wrong. It's no use pouting and crying; that won't repay the trouble I've had scouring the country after you. To think how Mr. Linton charged me to keep you in; and you stealing off so, it shows you are a cunning little fox, and nobody will put faith in you any more."

❦

CHARLES BAUDELAIRE
1821–1867

Charles Baudelaire was a French poet, essayist, translator and critic. His poetry is often associated with the flâneur figure, an idle, wealthy, urban explorer, and observer of city life. In his essay 'The Painter of Modern Life', he says that the flâneur walks in search of experience, crossing seamlessly between the outer world of public city spaces and the inner world of private passions. We see this idea powerfully portrayed in the following poem, 'To a Passer-by', from Baudelaire's collection *The Flowers of Evil* (first published in French in 1857). The narrator describes the thrill he feels when he walks past a beautiful woman, a moment that is intensely powerful, but unseen by the world around him.

'To a Passer-by'

Around me thundered the deafening noise of the street,
In mourning apparel, portraying majestic distress,
With queenly fingers, just lifting the hem of her dress,
A stately woman passed by with hurrying feet.

Agile and noble, with limbs of perfect poise,
Ah, how I drank, thrilled through like a Being insane,
In her look, a dark sky, from whence springs forth the
      hurricane,
There lay but the sweetness that charms, and the joy that
      destroys.

A flash—then the night . . . O loveliness fugitive!
Whose glance has so suddenly caused me again to live,
Shall I not see you again till this life is o'er!

Elsewhere, far away . . . too late, perhaps never more,
For I know not whither you fly, nor you, where I go,
O soul that I would have loved, and *that* you know!

A. E. HOUSMAN
1859–1936

Alfred Edward Housman was an English poet and an eminent scholar. He is best known for *A Shropshire Lad* (1896), a cycle of lyrical poems which are preoccupied with death, youth, love and disappointment, set to the backdrop of the English countryside. The collection has a melancholic, despairing tone, and the following poem, 'White in the moon the long road lies', is no exception. The narrator longs for his beloved, and tries to find hope in the thought of their eventual reunion. His poetry beautifully captures the meditative state that walking facilitates.

from 'White in the moon the long road lies'

White in the moon the long road lies,
    The moon stands blank above;
White in the moon the long road lies
    That leads me from my love.

Still hangs the hedge without a gust,
    Still, still the shadows stay:
My feet upon the moonlit dust
    Pursue the ceaseless way.

The world is round, so travellers tell,
    And straight though reach the track,
Trudge on, trudge on, 'twill all be well,
    The way will guide one back.

But ere the circle homeward hies
    Far, far must it remove:
White in the moon the long road lies
    That leads me from my love.

WILKIE COLLINS
1824–1889

Wilkie Collins was an English poet, playwright and novelist. He is best known for his novels *The Woman in White* (1859) and *The Moonstone* (1868). The following extract is from *Rambles Beyond Railways; or, Notes in Cornwall Taken A-foot* (1851), a travel narrative about Collins's walking tour of Cornwall at a time when the railways had not yet opened in that part of England. The book combines beautiful descriptions of scenery with digressions about Cornish history, folklore and manners. There is a sense of being 'off-grid' in the following extract, of being free from any kind of schedule. In a rapidly accelerating and commercialized world, the pedestrian is 'the free citizen of the whole travelling world', able to dictate their own pace. Nonetheless, there is a consciousness throughout the book that this hurry-free haven must eventually catch up with the rest of the world.

from *Rambles Beyond Railways*

II. A CORNISH FISHING-TOWN

The time is ten o'clock at night—the scene, a bank by the road-side, crested with young fir-trees, and affording a temporary place of repose to two travellers, who are enjoying the cool night air, picturesquely extended flat on their backs—or rather, on their knapsacks, which now form part and parcel of their backs. These two travellers are, the writer of this book, and an artist friend who is the companion of his rambles. They have long desired to explore Cornwall together, on foot; and the object of their aspirations has been at last accomplished, in the summer-time of the year eighteen hundred and fifty.

In their present position, the travellers are (to speak geographically) bounded towards the east by a long road winding down the side of a rocky hill; towards the west, by the broad half-dry channel of a tidal river; towards the north, by trees, hills, and upland valleys; and towards the south, by an old bridge and some houses near it, with lights in their windows faintly reflected in shallow water. In plainer words, the southern boundary of the prospect around them represents a place called Looe—a fishing-town on the south coast of Cornwall, which is their destination for the night.

They had, by this time, accomplished their initiation into the process of walking under a knapsack, with the most complete and encouraging success. You, who in these days of vehement bustle, business, and competition, can still find time to travel for pleasure alone—you, who have yet to become emancipated from the thraldom of railways, carriages, and saddle-horses—patronize, I exhort you, that first and oldest-established of all conveyances, your own legs! Think on your tender partings nipped in the bud by the railway bell; think of crabbed cross-roads, and broken carriage-springs; think of luggage confided to extortionate porters, of horses casting shoes and catching colds, of cramped legs and numbed feet, of vain longings to get down for a moment here, and to delay for a pleasant half hour there—think of all these manifold hardships of riding at your ease; and the next time you leave home, strap your luggage on your shoulders, take your stick in your hand, set forth delivered from a perfect paraphernalia of incumbrances, to go where you will, how you will—the free citizen of the whole travelling world! Thus independent, what may you not accomplish?—what pleasure is there that you cannot enjoy? Are you an artist?—you can stop to sketch every point of view that strikes your eye. Are you a philanthropist?—you can go into every cottage and talk to every human being you pass. Are you a botanist, or geologist?—you may pick up leaves and chip rocks wherever you please, the live-long day. Are you a valetudinarian?—you may physic yourself by Nature's own simple prescription, walking in fresh air. Are you dilatory and irresolute?—you may dawdle to your heart's content; you may change all your plans a dozen times in a dozen hours; you may tell "Boots" at the inn to call you at six o'clock, may fall asleep again (ecstatic sensation!) five minutes after he has knocked at the door, and may get up two hours later, to pursue your journey, with perfect impunity and satisfaction. For, to you, what is a time-table but waste-paper?—and a "booked place" but a relic of the dark ages? You dread, perhaps, blisters on your feet—sponge your feet with cold vinegar and water, change your socks every ten miles, and show me blisters after that, if you can! You strap on your knapsack for the first time, and five minutes afterwards feel an aching pain in the muscles at the back of your neck—walk *on*, and the aching will walk *off*! How do we overcome our first painful cuticular reminiscences of first getting on horseback?—by riding again. Apply the same rule to carrying the knapsack, and be assured of the same successful result. Again I say it, therefore—walk, and be merry; walk, and be healthy; walk, and be your own master!—walk, to enjoy, to observe, to improve, as no riders can!—walk, and you are the best peripatetic impersonation of holiday enjoyment that is to be met with on the surface of this work-a-day world!

How much more could I not say in praise of travelling on our own neglected legs? But it is getting late; dark night-clouds are marching slowly over the sky, to the whistling music of the wind; we must leave our bank by the road-side, pass one end of the old bridge, walk along a narrow winding street, and enter our hospitable little inn, where we are welcomed by the kindest of landladies, and waited on by the fairest of chambermaids. If Looe prove not to be a little sea-shore paradise to-morrow, then is there no virtue in the good omens of to-night.

❦

JANE AUSTEN
1775–1817

Jane Austen is one of the most eminent English novelists, famous for producing witty work that critiqued the lifestyles and values of the British landed gentry in her time. In this extract from her most famous novel *Pride and Prejudice* (1813), Elizabeth Bennet walks three miles to visit her sick sister, leaving her peers horrified that she, a respectable woman, has the nerve to walk such a distance 'so early in the day, in such dirty weather, and by herself'. Here, walking is a powerful rebellion against polite society and its suffocating etiquette.

from *Pride and Prejudice*

Mrs Bennet was prevented replying by the entrance of the footman with a note for Miss Bennet; it came from Netherfield, and the servant waited for an answer. Mrs Bennet's eyes sparkled with pleasure, and she was eagerly calling out, while her daughter read—

"Well, Jane, who is it from? what is it about? what does he say? Well, Jane, make haste and tell us; make haste, my love."

"It is from Miss Bingley," said Jane, and then read it aloud.

"MY DEAR FRIEND,—

"If you are not so compassionate as to dine to-day with Louisa and me, we shall be in danger of hating each other for the rest of our lives, for a whole day's tête-à-tête between two women can never end without a quarrel. Come as soon as you can on the receipt of this. My brother and the gentlemen are to dine with the officers.—Yours ever,   CAROLINE BINGLEY."

"With the officers!" cried Lydia. "I wonder my aunt did not tell us of *that*."

"Dining out," said Mrs Bennet, "that is very unlucky."

"Can I have the carriage?" said Jane.

"No, my dear, you had better go on horseback, because it seems likely to rain; and then you must stay all night."

"That would be a good scheme," said Elizabeth, "if you were sure that they would not offer to send her home."

"Oh! but the gentlemen will have Mr Bingley's chaise to go to Meryton; and the Hursts have no horses to theirs."

"I had much rather go in the coach."

"But, my dear, your father cannot spare the horses, I am sure. They are wanted in the farm, Mr Bennet, are not they?"

"They are wanted in the farm much oftener than I can get them."

"But if you have got them to-day," said Elizabeth, "my mother's purpose will be answered."

She did at last extort from her father an acknowledgment that the horses were engaged; Jane was therefore obliged to go on horseback, and her mother attended her to the door with many cheerful prognostics of a bad day. Her hopes were answered; Jane had not been gone long before it rained hard. Her sisters were uneasy for her, but her mother was delighted. The rain continued the whole evening without intermission; Jane certainly could not come back.

"This was a lucky idea of mine, indeed!" said Mrs Bennet more than once, as if the credit of making it rain were all her own. Till the next morning, however, she was not aware of all the felicity of her contrivance. Breakfast was scarcely over when a servant from Netherfield brought the following note for Elizabeth:—

"MY DEAREST LIZZY,—

"I find myself very unwell this morning, which, I suppose, is to be imputed to my getting wet through yesterday. My kind friends will not hear of my returning home till I am better. They insist also on my seeing Mr Jones—therefore do not be alarmed if you should hear of his having been to me—and, excepting a sore-throat and headache, there is not much the matter with me.—Yours, &c."

"Well, my dear," said Mr Bennet, when Elizabeth had read the note aloud, "if your daughter should have a dangerous fit of illness—if she should die, it would be a comfort to know that it was all in pursuit of Mr Bingley, and under your orders."

"Oh! I am not at all afraid of her dying. People do not die of little trifling colds. She will be taken good care of. As long as she stays there, it is all very well. I would go and see her if I could have the carriage."

Elizabeth, feeling really anxious, was determined to go to her, though the carriage was not to be had; and as she was no horsewoman, walking was her only alternative. She declared her resolution.

"How can you be so silly," cried her mother, "as to think of such a thing, in all this dirt! You will not be fit to be seen when you get there."

"I shall be very fit to see Jane—which is all I want."

"Is this a hint to me, Lizzy," said her father, "to send for the horses?"

"No, indeed. I do not wish to avoid the walk. The distance is nothing when one has a motive; only three miles. I shall be back by dinner."

"I admire the activity of your benevolence," observed Mary, "but every impulse of feeling should be guided by reason; and, in my opinion, exertion should always be in proportion to what is required."

"We will go as far as Meryton with you," said Catherine and Lydia. Elizabeth accepted their company, and the three young ladies set off together.

"If we make haste," said Lydia, as they walked along, "perhaps we may see something of Captain Carter before he goes."

In Meryton they parted; the two youngest repaired to the lodgings of one of the officer's wives, and Elizabeth continued her walk alone, crossing field after field at a quick pace, jumping over stiles and springing over puddles with impatient activity, and finding herself at last within view of the house, with weary ankles, dirty stockings, and a face glowing with the warmth of exercise.

She was shewn into the breakfast-parlour, where all but Jane were assembled, and where her appearance created a great deal of surprize. That she should have walked three miles so early in the day, in such dirty weather, and by herself, was almost incredible to Mrs Hurst and Miss Bingley; and Elizabeth was convinced that they held her in contempt for it. She was received, however, very politely by them; and in their brother's manners there was something better than politeness; there was good humour and kindness. Mr Darcy said very little, and Mr Hurst nothing at all. The former was divided between admiration of the brilliancy which exercise had given to her complexion, and doubt as to the occasion's justifying her coming so far alone. The latter was thinking only of his breakfast.

W. B. YEATS
1865–1939

William Butler Yeats was an Irish poet, dramatist, essayist and Nobel Prize winner. He was a key figure in the Irish Literary Revival, and accordingly his work is preoccupied with a search for Irish identity. In the next poem, 'The Song of Wandering Aengus', taken from his collection *The Wind Among the Reeds* (1899), a supernatural being appears to the mysterious figure Aengus out in the woods. The poem draws on ancient pagan beliefs, tying Irish identity to a mythological past and, more importantly, to the landscape. It creates a vision of Ireland that is taken from a primitive, rural, Celtic identity, convincing us that the 'real Ireland' can be discovered and known on foot.

'The Song of Wandering Aengus'

I went out to the hazel wood,
Because a fire was in my head,
And cut and peeled a hazel wand,
And hooked a berry to a thread;
And when white moths were on the wing,
And moth-like stars were flickering out,
I dropped the berry in a stream
And caught a little silver trout.

When I had laid it on the floor
I went to blow the fire a-flame,
But something rustled on the floor,
And someone called me by my name:
It had become a glimmering girl
With apple blossom in her hair
Who called me by my name and ran
And faded through the brightening air.

Though I am old with wandering
Through hollow lands and hilly lands,
I will find out where she has gone,
And kiss her lips and take her hands;
And walk among long dappled grass,
And pluck till time and times are done,
The silver apples of the moon,
The golden apples of the sun.

JOHN CLARE
1793–1864

John Clare was an English labouring-class Romantic poet whose work was primarily concerned with nature. In Clare's poems, walking is closely tied to paying attention. These poems are full of minute observations of the rural surroundings (as is to be expected from someone who worked out in the fields and knew the countryside intimately). Clare continued to farm even long after his poetry gained public recognition. His poems 'Summer Moods' and 'An Idle Hour' from the collection *The Rural Muse: Poems* (1835) paint remarkably detailed pictures of rural scenes. In these two we note a snail, the cry of a landrail (a type of bird), the ripple on a river, water droplets on leaves, and more.

'Summer Moods'

I love at even-tide to walk alone,
    Down narrow lanes o'erhung with dewy thorn,
Where from the long grass underneath, the snail
    Jet black creeps out and sprouts his timid horn.
I love to muse o'er meadows newly mown,
    Where withering grass perfumes the sultry air;
Where bees search round with sad and weary drone,
    In vain for flowers that bloomed but newly there;
While in the juicy corn, the hidden quail
    Cries "wet my foot!" and hid as thoughts unborn,
The fairy-like and seldom-seen landrail
    Utters "craik, craik," like voices underground:
Right glad to meet the evening's dewy veil,
    And see the light fade into glooms around.

'An Idle Hour'

Sauntering at ease, I often love to lean
    O'er old bridge walls, and mark the flood below,
Whose ripples, through the weeds of oily green,
    Like happy travellers chatter as they go;
And view the sunshine dancing on the arch,
    Time keeping to the merry waves beneath.
While on the banks some drooping blossoms parch,
    Thirsting for water in the day's hot breath,
Right glad of mud-drops splashed upon their leaves
    By cattle plunging from the steepy brink;
Each water-flower more than its share receives,
    And revels to its very cups in drink:—
So in the world, some strive, and fare but ill,
    While others riot, and have plenty still.

ROSA N. CAREY
1840–1909

Rosa Nouchette Carey was an English novelist and children's writer. She was extremely prolific, producing forty-one novels in total that were very popular with a certain portion of the reading public. Her work divided opinion, some viewing them as comically old-fashioned, others considering their wholesome nature a good influence on young girls. *Not Like Other Girls* (1884) is a novel about three genteel sisters who, finding themselves bankrupt, begin their own dressmaking business – the dictum of the novel being that, despite common opinion, it is in fact possible, even admirable, for the gentry to work if they need to. Going out walking becomes a haven for secret intimacy in a society where young people's behaviour was strictly monitored. In the following extract, we learn that for the young lovers Dick and Nan, going walking is not about walking; the apparently keen walker Dick fails to be excited by the prospect of a summer in the Alps because it means that he'll miss his daily rambles with Nan in their humble neighbourhood.

from *Not Like Other Girls*

CHAPTER II.

DICK OBJECTS TO THE MOUNTAINS.

'Shall we have our usual stroll?' asked Phillis, as Nan and Dick joined her at the window.

This was one of the customs at Glen Cottage. When any such fitting escort offered itself, the three girls would put on their hats, and, regardless of the evening dews and their crisp white dresses, would saunter, under Dick's guidance, through the quiet village, or down and up the country roads, 'just for a breath of air,' as they would say.

It is only fair to Mrs. Challoner's views of propriety to say that she would have trusted her three pretty daughters to no other young man but Dick; and of late certain prudential doubts had crossed her mind. It was all very well for Phillis to say Dick was Dick, and there was an end of it. After all he belonged to the phalanx of her enemies, those shadowy invaders of her hearth who threatened her maternal peace. Dick was not a boy any longer; he had outgrown his hobbledehoy ways; the slight sandy moustache that he so proudly caressed was not a greater proof of his manhood than the undefinable change that had passed over his manners.

Mrs. Challoner began to distrust these evening

strolls, and to turn over in her own mind various wary pretexts for detaining Nan on the next occasion.

'Just this once, perhaps, it does not matter,' she murmured to herself, as she composed herself for her usual nap.

'We shall not be long, little mother, so you must not be dull,' Dulce had said, kissing her lightly over her eyes. This was just one of the pleasant fictions at the cottage—one of those graceful little deceptions that are so harmless in families.

Dulce knew of those placid after-dinner naps. She knew her mother's eyes would only unclose when Dorothy brought in the tea-tray; but she was also conscious that nothing would displease her mother more than to notice this habit. When they lingered indoors, and talked in whispers so as not to disturb her, Mrs. Challoner had an extraordinary facility for striking into the conversation in a way that was somewhat confusing.

'I don't agree with you at all,' she would say, in a drowsy voice. 'Is it not time for Dorothy to bring in the tea? I wish you would all talk louder. I must be getting a little deaf, I think, for I don't hear half you say.'

'Oh, it was only nonsense talk, mammie,' Dulce would answer; and the sisterly chitchat would recommence, and her mother's head nid-nodded on the cushions until the next interruption.

'We shall not have many more of these strolls,' observed Dick regretfully, as they all walked together through the village, and then branched off into a long country road, where the air blew freshly in their faces, and low mists hung over the meadow-land. Though it was not quite dark, there was a tiny moon, and the glimmer of a star or two; and there was a pleasant fragrance as of new-mown grass.

They were all walking abreast, and keeping step, and Dick was in the middle, with Nan beside him. Dulce was hanging on her arm, and every now and then breaking into little snatches of song.

'How I envy you!' exclaimed Phillis. 'Think of spending three whole months in Switzerland! Oh, you lucky Dick!'

For the Maynes had decided to pass the long vacation in the Engadine. Some hints had been dropped that Nan should accompany them, but Mrs. Challoner had regarded the invitation with some disfavour, and Mrs. Mayne had not pressed the point. If only Nan had known! but her mother had in this matter kept her own counsel.

'I don't know about that,' dissented Dick; he was rather given to argue for the mere pleasure of oppos- ition. 'Mountains and glaciers are all very well in their way; but I think, on the whole, I would as soon be here. You see I am so accustomed to mix with a lot of fellows, that I am afraid of finding the pater's sole company rather slow.'

'For shame!' remarked his usual monitress. But she spoke gently; in her heart she knew why Dick failed to find the mountains alluring.

GEORGE ELIOT
1819–1880

Mary Ann Evans, best known by her pen name
George Eliot, was a leading Victorian novelist, poet
and journalist born in Warwickshire, England. Her
realist novels are widely recognized as pioneering the
subjective, psychological interiority which would
later characterize Modern fiction. In this extract from
Middlemarch (1872), Eliot expertly weaves her protagonist Dorothea Brooke's interior and exterior
worlds as she walks through the woods and contem-
plates her future. Going out walking allows Dorothea
to enter a space where she is free of the expectations
of the Middlemarch community – though unfortu-
nately in this case, the thoughts of our ascetic heroine
lead her to choose a miserable path involving the
much older, solemn scholar, Casaubon.

from *Middlemarch*

It was three o'clock in the beautiful breezy autumn day when Mr Casaubon drove off to his Rectory at Lowick, only five miles from Tipton; and Dorothea, who had on her bonnet and shawl, hurried along the shrubbery and across the park that she might wander through the bordering wood with no other visible companionship than that of Monk, the Great St Bernard dog, who always took care of the young ladies in their walks. There had risen before her the girl's vision of a possible future for herself to which she looked forward with trembling hope, and she wanted to wander on in that visionary future without interruption. She walked briskly in the brisk air, the colour rose in her cheeks, and her straw-bonnet (which our contemporaries might look at with conjectural curiosity as at an obsolete form of basket) fell a little backward. She would perhaps be hardly characterised enough if it were omitted that she wore her brown hair flatly braided and coiled behind so as to expose the outline of her head in a daring manner at a time when public feeling required the meagreness of nature to be dissimulated by tall barricades of frizzed curls and bows, never surpassed by any great race except the Feejeean. This was a trait of Miss Brooke's asceticism. But there was nothing of an ascetic's expression in her bright full eyes, as she looked before her, not consciously seeing, but absorbing into the intensity of her mood, the solemn glory of the afternoon with its long swathes of light between the far-off rows of limes, whose shadows touched each other.

All people, young or old (that is, all people in those ante-reform times), would have thought her an interesting object if they had referred the glow in her eyes and cheeks to the newly-awakened ordinary images of young love: the illusions of Chloe about Strephon have been sufficiently consecrated in poetry, as the pathetic loveliness of all spontaneous trust ought to be. Miss Pippin adoring young Pumpkin, and dreaming along endless vistas of unwearying companionship, was a little drama which never tired our fathers and mothers, and had been put into all costumes. Let but Pumpkin have a figure which would sustain the disadvantages of the short-waisted swallow-tail, and everybody felt it not only natural but necessary to the perfection of womanhood, that a sweet girl should be at once convinced of his virtue, his exceptional ability, and above all, his perfect sincerity. But perhaps no persons then living—certainly none in the neighbourhood of Tipton—would have had a sympathetic understanding for the dreams of a girl whose notions about marriage took their colour entirely from an exalted enthusiasm about the ends of life, an enthusiasm which was lit chiefly by its own fire, and included neither the niceties of the *trousseau*, the pattern of plate, nor even the honours and sweet joys of the blooming matron.

It had now entered Dorothea's mind that Mr Casaubon might wish to make her his wife, and the idea that he would do so touched her with a sort of reverential gratitude. How good of him—nay, it would be almost as if a winged messenger had suddenly stood beside her path and held out his hand towards her! For a long while she had been oppressed by the indefiniteness which hung in her mind, like a thick summer haze, over all her desire to make her life greatly effective. What could she do, what ought she to do?—she, hardly more than a budding woman, but yet with an active conscience and a great mental need, not to be satisfied by a girlish instruction comparable to the nibblings and judgments of a discursive mouse. With some endowment of stupidity and conceit, she might have thought that a Christian young lady of fortune should find her ideal of life in village charities, patronage of the humbler clergy, the perusal of 'Female Scripture Characters,' unfolding the private experience of Sara under the Old Dispensation, and

Dorcas under the New, and the care of her soul over her embroidery in her own boudoir—with a background of prospective marriage to a man who, if less strict than herself, as being involved in affairs religiously inexplicable, might be prayed for and seasonably exhorted. From such contentment poor Dorothea was shut out. The intensity of her religious disposition, the coercion it exercised over her life, was but one aspect of a nature altogether ardent, theoretic, and intellectually consequent: and with such a nature struggling in the bands of a narrow teaching, hemmed in by a social life which seemed nothing but a labyrinth of petty courses, a walled-in maze of small paths that led no whither, the outcome was sure to strike others as at once exaggeration and inconsistency. The thing which seemed to her best, she wanted to justify by the completest knowledge; and not to live in a pretended admission of rules which were never acted on. Into this soul-hunger as yet all her youthful passion was poured; the union which attracted her was one that would deliver her from her girlish subjection to her own ignorance, and give her the freedom of voluntary submission to a guide who would take her along the grandest path.

"I should learn everything then," she said to herself, still walking quickly along the bridle road through the wood. "It would be my duty to study that I might help him the better in his great works. There would be nothing trivial about our lives. Everyday-things with us would mean the greatest things. It would be like marrying Pascal. I should learn to see the truth by the same light as great men have seen it by. And then I should know what to do, when I got older: I should see how it was possible to lead a grand life here—now—in England. I don't feel sure about doing good in any way now: everything seems like going on a mission to a people whose language I don't know;—unless it were building good cottages—there can be no doubt about that. Oh, I hope I should be able to get the people well housed in Lowick! I will draw plenty of plans while I have time."

JOHN DYER
1699–1757

John Dyer was a Welsh poet, painter and priest. The
following poem 'The Country Walk' records a stroll
on Grongar Hill in Carmarthenshire. We may detect
his painter's eye in his descriptions of the landscape:
his attention to light, shade, colour. We may also
notice that the classical references transfigure the
humble walker into a hero of mythology and Grongar Hill into Mount Helicon. This delight and pride
in his native landscape would later inspire the likes
of William Wordsworth.

'The Country Walk'

The morning's fair; the lusty sun
With ruddy cheek begins to run,
And early birds, that wing the skies,
Sweetly sing to see him rise.

    I am resolv'd, this charming day,
In the open field to stray,
And have no roof above my head,
But that whereon the gods do tread.
Before the yellow barn I see
A beautiful variety
Of strutting cocks, advancing stout,
And flirting empty chaff about:
Hens, ducks, and geese, and all their brood,
And turkeys gobbling for their food,
While rustics thrash the wealthy floor,
And tempt all to crowd the door.

    What a fair face does Nature show!
Augusta! wipe thy dusty brow;
A landscape wide salutes my sight
Of shady vales and mountains bright;
And azure heavens I behold,
And clouds of silver and of gold.
And now into the fields I go,
Where thousand flaming flowers glow,
And every neighb'ring hedge I greet,

With honey-suckles smelling sweet.
Now o'er the daisy-meads I stray,
And meet with, as I pace my way,
Sweetly shining on the eye,
A riv'let gliding smoothly by,
Which shows with what an easy tide
The moments of the happy glide:
Here, finding pleasure after pain,
Sleeping, I see a weary'd swain,
While his full scrip lies open by,
That does his healthy food supply.

Happy swain! sure happier far
Than lofty kings and princes are!
Enjoy sweet sleep, which shuns the crown,
With all its easy beds of down.

The sun now shows his noon-tide blaze,
And sheds around me burning rays.
A little onward, and I go
Into the shade that groves bestow,
And on green moss I lay me down,
That o'er the root of oak has grown;
Where all is silent, but some flood,
That sweetly murmurs in the wood;
But birds that warble in the sprays,
And charm ev'n Silence with their lays.

Oh! pow'rful Silence! how you reign
In the poet's busy brain!

His num'rous thoughts obey the calls
  Of the tuneful waterfalls;
Like moles, whene'er the coast is clear,
They rise before thee without fear,
And range in parties here and there.

  Some wildly to Parnassus wing,
And view the fair Castalian spring,
Where they behold a lonely well
Where now no tuneful Muses dwell,
But now and then a slavish hind
Paddling the troubled pool they find.

  Some trace the pleasing paths of joy,
Others the blissful scene destroy,
In thorny tracks of sorrow stray,
And pine for Clio far away.
But stay—Methinks her lays I hear,
So smooth! so sweet! so deep! so clear!
No, it is not her voice I find;
'Tis but the echo stays behind.

  Some meditate Ambition's brow,
And the black gulf that gapes below;
Some peep in courts, and there they see
The sneaking tribe of Flattery:
But, striking to the ear and eye,
A nimble deer comes bounding by!
When rushing from yon rustling spray
It made them vanish all away.

I rouse me up, and on I rove;
'Tis more than time to leave the grove.
The sun declines, the evening breeze
Begins to whisper thro' the trees;
And as I leave the sylvan gloom,
As to the glare of day I come,
An old man's smoky nest I see
Leaning on an aged tree,
Whose willow walls, and furzy brow,
A little garden sway below:
Thro' spreading beds of blooming green,
Matted with herbage sweet and clean,
A vein of water limps along,
And makes them ever green and young.
Here he puffs upon his spade,
And digs up cabbage in the shade:
His tatter'd rags are sable brown,
His beard and hair are hoary grown;
The dying sap descends apace,
And leaves a wither'd hand and face.

Up Grongar Hill I labour now,
And catch at last his bushy brow.
Oh! how fresh, how pure, the air!
Let me breathe a little here.
Where am I, Nature? I descry
Thy magazine before me lie.
Temples!—and towns!—and towers!—and woods!—

And hills!—and vales!—and fields!—and floods!
Crowding before me, edg'd around
With naked wilds and barren ground.

See, below, the pleasant dome,
The poet's pride, the poet's home,
Which the sunbeams shine upon
To the even from the dawn.
See her woods, where Echo talks,
Her gardens trim, her terrace walks,
Her wildernesses, fragrant brakes,
Her gloomy bow'rs and shining lakes.
Keep, ye Gods! this humble seat
For ever pleasant, private, neat.

See yonder hill, uprising steep,
Above the river slow and deep;
It looks from hence a pyramid,
Beneath a verdant forest hid;
On whose high top there rises great
The mighty remnant of a seat,
An old green tow'r, whose batter'd brow
Frowns upon the vale below.

Look upon that flow'ry plain,
How the sheep surround their swain,
How they crowd to hear his strain!
All careless with his legs across,
Leaning on a bank of moss,
He spends his empty hours at play,

Which fly as light as down away.

    And there behold a bloomy mead,
A silver stream, a willow shade,
Beneath the shade a fisher stand,
Who, with the angle in his hand,
Swings the nibbling fry to land.

    In blushes the descending sun
Kisses the streams, while slow they run;
And yonder hill remoter grows,
Or dusky clouds do interpose.
The fields are left, the labouring hind
His weary oxen does unbind;
And vocal mountains, as they low,
Re-echo to the vales below;
The jocund shepherds piping come,
And drive the herd before them home;
And now begin to light their fires,
Which send up smoke in curling spires;
While with light hearts all homeward tend,
To Aberglasney I descend.

    But, oh! how bless'd would be the day
Did I with Clio pace my way,
And not alone and solitary stray.

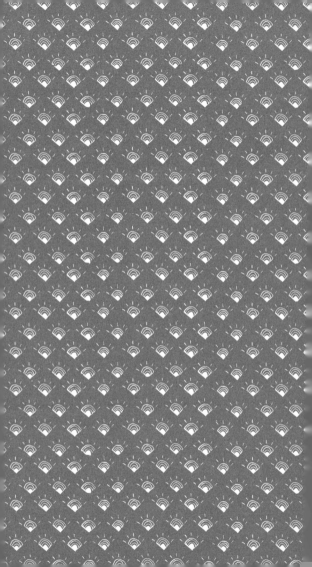